Something Was Rotten
in the State of Ohio.

With fifteen seconds to go in the last quarter of Globe University's football game, the Monarchs remained scoreless against the Fortinbras U.'s Fighting Generals. Cameron Dean, star quarterback of the Monarchs, faced his first loss in three seasons. Fifteen seconds and twenty yards to go, fourth down. This wouldn't just be a loss, it'd be an upset. Even "upset" would be putting it mildly, "embarrassment" a vast understatement.

And the ghost—or was it a demon?—that was haunting the goal line wasn't making things any easier. . . .

BARD'S BLOOD #1
HAMLET II
OPHELIA'S REVENGE

A NOVEL BY DAVID BERGANTINO
BASED ON *THE TRAGEDY OF HAMLET, PRINCE OF DENMARK*
BY WILLIAM SHAKESPEARE

POCKET STAR BOOKS
New York   London   Toronto   Sydney   Singapore

The sale of this book without its cover is unauthorized. If you purchased this book without a cover, you should be aware that it was reported to the publisher as "unsold and destroyed." Neither the author nor the publisher has received payment for the sale of this "stripped book."

This book is a work of fiction. Names, characters, places and incidents are products of the author's imagination or are used fictitiously. Any resemblance to actual events or locales or persons, living or dead, is entirely coincidental.

An *Original* Publication of POCKET BOOKS

A Pocket Star Book published by
POCKET BOOKS, a division of Simon & Schuster, Inc.
1230 Avenue of the Americas, New York, NY 10020

Copyright © 2003 by David Bergantino

All rights reserved, including the right to reproduce
this book or portions thereof in any form whatsoever.
For information address Pocket Books, 1230 Avenue
of the Americas, New York, NY 10020

ISBN: 0-7434-5624-6

First Pocket Books printing February 2003

10 9 8 7 6 5 4 3 2 1

POCKET STAR BOOKS and colophon are registered
trademarks of Simon & Schuster, Inc.

For information regarding special discounts for bulk purchases,
please contact Simon & Schuster Special Sales at 1-800-456-6798
or business@simonandschuster.com

Front cover illustration by Jerry Vanderstelt

Printed in the U.S.A.

With thanks and apologies to
William Shakespeare,
who never went Hollywood.

HAMLET II
OPHELIA'S REVENGE

1

Something was rotten in the state of Ohio.

With fifteen seconds to go in the last quarter of Globe University's football game, the Monarchs remained scoreless against the Fortinbras U.'s Fighting Generals. Cameron Dean, star quarterback of the Monarchs, faced his first loss in three seasons. Fifteen seconds and twenty yards to go, fourth down. This wouldn't just be a loss, it'd be an upset. Even "upset" would be putting it too mildly, "embarrassment" a vast understatement.

The Monarchs had marched up and down the field at will for most of the game, running roughshod over the Fortinbras defense. Despite this domination, the end zone itself seemed to be surrounded by an impenetrable force field. Bobbled passes, fumbles, tangled legs and more, all this from the strongest offense in the division three years running, kept even a field goal out of the Monarchs' reach. The Fighting

Generals had scored their one touchdown on a ninety-eight yard runback due to one of these incredible mishaps. The dozen or so Fortinbras fans in the bleachers were so stunned they nearly forgot to cheer. Surely a penalty would be called to bring the ball back. It was like that for the Fighting Generals. But this time, luck was on their side. The touchdown counted, the extra point easily scored and amazingly, the Fighting Generals seemed poised to defeat the supposedly invincible Monarchs.

Fifteen seconds and twenty yards to go, fourth down. Behind by seven points. Yes, something was more than rotten in the state of Ohio, specifically, the college town of Stratford. Said rottenness emanated pungently from Globe University's football field, and it wasn't fresh mulch.

Cameron used the team's last time out for a quick huddle. As he approached, he ripped off his helmet and threw it to the ground. It landed spinning, a red-and-gold blur, at the feet of a squat player, Jackson Pierson, his center.

"What the fuck, guys?" Cameron yelled. "Whatever your problems have been for the last couple hours, you better get over them real quick. Like *right* now!" One by one he examined each teammate with furious blue eyes. Most looked down or away, riddled with shame. Cameron shook his head in disgust. "It would be bad enough to lose, in front of our families, in front of our girlfriends, in front of ourselves, for

God's sake, on any other game, but it's Fortinbras." He nearly choked. "Fuckin' Fortinbras Fighting *Privates!* You wanna lose to those pussies?!"

Helmets shaking side to side. Murmurs rippling through the huddle, glances exchanged.

"What the hell kind of response is that? Did body snatchers land last night and replace *my* team with a bunch of pussies?"

No one in the team would look at Cameron directly. They all seemed to be glancing at either Marc or Bernie. Marc Borkowski and Bernie Genova were Cameron's wide receivers. God had built the two big, strong and quick. But today, he had seen fit to remove their coordination. In every other game, the two seemed to have flypaper embedded in their palms. Tonight, they could barely remain standing long enough to catch the ball, let alone hold on to it tightly when they did.

Right now, it appeared there was something to say and the rest of the team had elected the pair to say it.

"All right," Cameron said, staring directly at the two. "What is it?"

"Dude." Bernie struggled to speak. "It's your dad."

"Bernie and me," Marc continued, his voice shaking, "We saw . . . we saw your dad. In the end zone."

"My father's . . ." Cameron let his voice trail off. He could barely comprehend what he was hearing, in the middle of the huddle, at the end of a game they were just about to lose.

"Yeah, we know," Marc said softly. "That's the problem. We were tossing the ball around late the last few nights, getting psyched for the game like we do, and he was just . . . there. It was scary, dude. He looked . . . angry, or hungry . . . or something. It wasn't good, dude. Freaked us out. He might still be there. We . . . we don't wanna see him again."

Although he wasn't falling, wasn't afraid of heights, and had never experienced it in his life, Cameron suddenly felt vertigo. Marc's face, twitching with fear and embarrassment, seemed to draw closer and more clear in detail, while his surroundings seemed to suddenly recede in the distance.

Bernie looked toward the ground.

Cameron was livid, a bundle of frayed wires spitting electricity.

"We have a game to win against one of the lamest teams in the division." His voice was low and hissing. "It's a fucking home game, and I don't care if fucking Godzilla is tromping around making the end zone a radioactive wasteland. You're gonna go there, wait for the ball and catch it when I throw it to you and win this fucking game!"

Everyone took note. Cameron wasn't one to curse, even though he had been on edge for the last few weeks since his father's sudden death.

"Forget about my father," he told them, his voice restrained. "Forget about ghosts, forget about everything except *winning . . . this . . . game.*"

Cameron thrust his hand into the middle of the circle of players.

"Are you with me?" he cried suddenly.

The others paused for a moment, as if touching Cameron's hand would cause them to explode. Then suddenly, they remembered what they were doing there. Hands joined his, one after another, until they were one big mass of fingers. The chanting began.

"WOOFwoofwoofwoofWOOFwoofwoof . . ." Over and over again. The joined hands rose as one to the sky.

"Let's save this game!" Cameron cried, leading the team back to the field. The players followed, clearly energized. Cameron relaxed a little. He had them back. Or so it seemed. He hoped Marc and Bernie had overcome their momentary insanity. He'd know shortly.

At the line of scrimmage, the Monarchs' offense weren't the only ones looking stoked. The Fighting Generals were fifteen seconds away from knocking the Monarchs down a few pegs. Cameron watched the blitz form, but from the looks on the faces of the newly confident Generals, some players were going for more than the sack. They were going for the kill.

As he prepared to take the snap, Cameron could smell the smoke of wood fires common in a Midwestern October evening. He breathed deeply. The smoky air was nonetheless crisp. Time to find his winning place, the one deep in his mind, the one that only he could understand. The one that scared people when he went there, as he often did in times of pressure. It's how he coped. It's how he overcame. It's how he won. And he would win this one. As he always did. And not his grief over the death of his father, the bizarre claims of Marc and Bernie, not the unexpected relationship between his mother and his aunt, his father's sister, would distract him from his goal. He wouldn't just tie this game. He would win.

The snap. Cameron took the ball and faded back. The blitz was on something fierce. Fortinbras chewed up his protection instantly. Bernie went wide left, Marc drove straight down the middle. One pump—then a dodge. A hulking Fortinbras player dived at Cameron, who narrowly avoided being taken out. That would have ended the game. The quarterback's blues eyes only flicked briefly at the incoming monster, but it was enough. The landscape changed by the time he looked up again. Bernie's arc had taken him right out of bounds. He was no longer eligible to receive. Cameron turned back to Marc, who turned as he entered the end zone. He nearly threw the ball at that point, even as he dodged a second Fortinbras lineman. In the next moment, Marc collapsed in a sizeable heap in the end zone. There wasn't one Fortinbras player near him.

His best receivers down, his protection destroyed, Cameron suddenly found himself surrounded by dark blue uniforms. Mean, cruel eyes glared out from the helmets. It was over. The clock was ticking. He was done for, defeated and embarrassed in front of his whole school.

And then the landscape changed again. The blue sea parted somehow and Cameron could see the end zone again. Unfortunately, there was no red in the end zone, and from the looks of things, there wouldn't be. He had no time to think, only to act. Cameron ran forward, jumped an opponent who tried to bear-hug his legs, shrugged off another General who grabbed for his jersey, and he was through.

The crowd roared as they saw their quarterback, Cameron Dean, weave through the Fortinbras defense and run into the end zone. They were on their feet, cheering, yelling, stomping, as Cameron spiked the ball, making the score 6–7. Red uniforms suddenly pressed against him. He pushed them away. Whistles were blowing.

Marc sat up groggily as officials surrounded him. A trollish man, in too-short shorts despite the chill of the air, trotted out from the sidelines. Cameron pushed his way through the crowd.

"Marc?"

At the sound of his name, Marc's head snapped quickly left and right as if he were expecting to be attacked.

"It's me, Cameron." He knelt beside his fallen teammate. "You okay?"

As Marc got his bearings, a gruff voice bellowed, "What the hell, Borkowski?" The troll was Coach

Teren, poster child for the "Those Who Can't, Teach" philosophy.

Marc, now blinking slowly, peered from a mile behind his eyes.

"He passed out or something," Cameron said. Medical personnel were helping Marc onto a stretcher.

"Um, Coach?" came a weak voice. Bernie limped over from the sidelines. "I twisted my ankle on that last play. Um, I need to sit out too." His voice sounded more weak from embarrassment than from pain.

"What the hell, Genova?" Teren was turning purple with rage and confusion. "What the hell is going on?" He looked close to striking Bernie and giving him a good reason to sit out the crucial last play of the game. Clearly, Bernie had lost his nerve.

"Sub in your players and let's get this show on the road, Coach," said a thin, wrinkled official.

"Dammit!" Teren said to no one in particular, then turned sharply to Cameron. "Who do you want?" Teren deferred to Cameron's judgment in the heat of a game.

"Gimme Rosenberg and Gyllenhal," Cameron said without hesitation.

"The freshmen?" spat Teren. His purple deepened. "But Rosenberg and Gyllenhal are losers."

"It won't matter now. I just need the bodies."

Teren gulped air, then made an effort to calm himself down. "Okay, Cam. Win me this freakin' game, would ya?"

"That's what they pay me for!" Cameron replied. Teren barked a short laugh.

Moments later, Rosenberg and Gyllenhal jumped up from the bench, high-fived each other and scampered onto the field for the extra point play. They made a beeline for Cameron.

"Oh, man, thanks!" Ben Rosenberg said, almost giddy. His cheeks were ruddy with excitement, his breath coming out in ragged gasps. His face nearly matched his hair, a flame red that peeked from beneath his helmet.

"You totally rock!" Pete Gyllenhal told Cameron, patting him on the back before he, too, pulled on his helmet.

Cameron laughed. This was why he brought them out. As useless as the two freshmen were as players, Cameron needed their enthusiasm, their honest effort, and, yes, their hero worship to break the tension that had built up around the game. He knew that even if he lost the game, despite what anyone else would say, these two would remember that he asked them to play.

"About time you guys saw some action," he told them as they approached the line of scrimmage. He laughed again, their puppy-dog eyes regarding him with awe. It sure beat the hangdog expression on the faces of his remaining teammates.

"You won't regret it, Cam," said Gyllenhal.

"Yeah, Cam," said Rosenberg. "We got your back!"

Nodding to the freshmen in encouragement, he sharpened his focus on the next four seconds. He hurried his team into formation. The hell with the tie; he was going for the two-point conversion to win. Fortinbras was expecting this and lined up to stop him.

Pierson snapped the ball. Cameron held it, looking for a receiver. Rosenberg and Gyllenhal were flattened immediately by the Fortinbras defense. Other than that, the Globe line held better this time, but no one came open. Only one thing to do: run it in himself. But there was a solid wall of players before him, red jerseys meeting blue jerseys, with neither making much progress. If he tried to run around the group, he might shift the balance of power and be caught, losing the game instead of having gone for the safe tie.

Unacceptable.

Then he saw it, a white number 21 on a red jersey, at a forty-five degree angle to the turf. Rosenberg was rising to his feet. Immediately, a General tried to get past him. This time, Rosenberg held his ground. Beyond Rosenberg: the end zone.

Again, no thought, just action. Cameron sprang forward. Leaping, he planted his right foot solidly on Rosenberg's back and launched himself into the air. Hands reached up and scraped against his cleats as he sailed overhead. A moment later, Cameron landed and continued without breaking stride. Fortinbras didn't have a chance in hell to catch him. Again,

Cameron found himself in the end zone. This time, he held the ball aloft as the crowd roared. He filtered them out, listening for a whistle that would ruin everything. It did not come. The play had been good, no flags. Two points.

The Monarchs had just won, 8–7.

Cameron pumped the ball into the air and shouted.

As he drew in his breath for another cheer, a blue blur struck him from the side. Cameron lost consciousness before he hit the ground.

2

He was back in a huddle. The smell of smoke was strong now, nearly suffocating. Around him, the horizon was ablaze, smoke billowing into the air. The entire town was on fire and the football field was in the eye of the firestorm. This didn't seem to bother the fans cheering crazily from the stands. They ignored the danger, or somehow couldn't sense it.

"Pay attention, Cameron," shouted a voice. Cameron snapped his head back into the huddle. The voice belonged to his father, Cameron, Sr. The recently deceased.

"Dad . . . ? How . . . ?" young Cameron began. His voice and his thoughts oozed thickly. Before him stood his father. They were very similar, sharing intense blue eyes, broad shoulders and a lean, athletic build. Both had blond hair, although Cameron Sr.'s had dulled to a dishwater shade in his forties. Strangely, his father was wearing the uniform of the

Globe U. Monarchs from the seventies, the days when he had been quarterback.

"Focus, Cam!" his father snapped. "This is an important game. They're winning, and we can't let them win. Right?"

Other voices shouted in affirmation, but not all of the responses were in English. Cameron suddenly became aware of the others in the huddle. Across from him was an ancient man; thin, grizzled and wearing a tweed smoking jacket. On his face was the livid purple patch of a birthmark. It took up most of his right cheek. Cameron then noticed the man was looking blankly just to the right of Cameron's face. He realized the man was blind.

His other "teammates" were of various ages and wore different uniforms. Unlike his father, these were apparently military garb; some even wore armor. Next to Cameron—too close, he thought—was another strange character: a boy, in his late teens at best. From underneath a gold crown, the boy regarded Cameron fearfully with dark eyes that were nonetheless powerful and brooding. Cameron looked him over, puzzled at the velvet tunic the boy was wearing. The real shock for Cameron was below the boy's waist.

The two shared a pair of legs.

Cameron uttered a small cry and tried to pull away. This only succeeded in causing him to lose balance. The two boys' torsos seemed to be grafted at the waist. They waved four arms to regain balance and finally steadied themselves. The younger boy scolded him with his eyes.

"Daa-aa-aad?!" He felt like a panicky ten-year-old.

"You've got a Siamese soul, Cam," his father explained. "Some souls get passed from body to body. Others evolve or split off from other souls, sort of like cells dividing. That's how the population of the world can continue to grow, and everyone still gets a soul." He laughed darkly. "Doesn't stop people from acting soulless, of course. Anyway, your soul is sort of stuck in between, arrested before you could completely split off."

Cameron regarded his father, the other men in the huddle, and examined his own bizarrely formed body once more. Finally, he said: "I'm knocked out, right? I'm just hallucinating."

His father sighed and shook his head slowly. "It's a draw play, Cam. Sometimes you fake left, sometimes you fake right. This time, you've just faked 'in,' that's all. Now shut up and listen, there isn't much time."

Cameron, Sr.'s eyes reflected the fire. He was right; there wasn't much time. In the bleachers, the screaming fans caught fire. They didn't run, however, and seemed not to be in pain. They appeared only to be trying to shout over the roar of the flames that had begun to consume them. The fire crawled from riser to riser, from the top bench on down. Burning arms waved burning flags clutched in burning hands.

"My death was a draw play, too," his father continued, oblivious of the conflagration around them. "A total fake *out!*"

"But who . . . ?" Cameron could still barely form a thought, let alone a sentence. The fire, the smoke, the screaming—his senses threatened to shut down. The old man made a sharp noise, apparently intending for Cameron to shut up and listen to his father. His "Siamese twin" agreed, nodding gravely.

"Over there. The *other* team." Cameron's father's voice dripped with poison. He pointed. There, in pink uniforms, were his mother, Geri, looking strangely blank, and next to her, his father's sister, Claudia. They were surrounded by nine other figures, all dressed as strangely and variously as the men surrounding Cameron. Some weren't even human. Cameron saw a turtle and a lizard, each the size of a human, on the other team; they also wore pink uniforms. Aunt Claudia was clearly the quarterback, barking out orders to her team.

By now, the fire had consumed the bleachers entirely. Flames now ringed the field. The goalposts caught and quickly went up like torches.

"My sister is a clever one. Called a brilliant shotgun play and took me out of the game. But it's not just me. It's all the men in our family. We're cursed. Mainly because of this jerk." He stabbed a thumb at Cameron's twin, who stared back defiantly but said nothing. "You have to stop it. You have to stop her."

That's when Cameron noticed that his father's lips had drawn back in a frozen expression of death. He had looked like that when Cameron had found him in the study, on the floor behind his desk, covered in glass and dirt from the terrarium he had pulled down with him as he fell. At the time, Cameron had thought bizarrely of the game, Clue. Mr. Dean in the study with the revolver. Except there was no revolver; Mr. Dean had had a heart attack. And Mr. Dean wasn't a fictional character, but his own father. Clinging to the Clue image protected him long enough to call an ambulance. After that, he had fallen apart. And quite profoundly, it now seemed he was himself a sideshow freak, and being told by his dead father that he had been murdered.

"Aunt Claudia killed you?" asked Cameron. "Does Mom know?"

After his father's death, his aunt Claudia had taken over his father's position as president of Globe University. But she hadn't just filled his shoes in that regard; she had also stepped into her brother's bedroom slippers. Aunt Claudia was now also the "man" of the family, and had become her mother's domineering live-in lover.

"Darn tootin' she knew, kiddo," Cameron's father answered. "She let it happen."

"How could she?" Cameron asked.

"You know I love—loved—your mom, but she's a sucker for a strong personality." He shrugged. "But forget about her. No matter what you find out, no matter how you feel, leave your mom out of it. She's on someone else's task list. It's your aunt you have to take care of."

The goalposts collapsed in each end zone. Fire raced from either side toward both teams.

"What do you mean?"

His father just looked grim.

"Vengeance, Cam."

Cameron was suddenly aware that the fire had reached the huddle. In the distance, the women's team caught fire. Their burning bodies ran in small circles before collapsing in heaps on the field. The turtle flipped onto its back, its legs flailing until it finally died. Soon, only the lizard remained, not dying from the flames that engulfed it, but dancing about playfully, as a dolphin plays in the ocean's spray.

"Good old-fashioned vengeance, my son. That's what I mean." His lips didn't move. The sound simply emanated from him, as if he were wearing a death mask. A trickle of blood ran from his scalp, down across his lips and dripped off his chin.

More fire leapt at the men's team, beginning to consume them. The old man started screaming in his strange language. The fire reached his father and started climbing his legs.

"Dad, come on!" He tugged at his father's shoulder but it was like pulling on a stone monument. The boy beside Cameron remained passive.

"Play clock is running out, son," said his father. The blood on his face started sizzling as his shoulder pads caught fire. "You gotta win this!"

Then his father became a column of fire. Still, he did not run. He did not scream. And the last thing Cameron heard, through the crackling flames was: "Avenge my death!"

"Daaaaaddddd!!!" Cameron screamed as his father blew away in a cloud of fireflies.

And then he was drowning. Water filled his mouth, still open from screaming, and sought to settle in his lungs. Choking, Cameron sat up suddenly, his forehead connecting with something hard. A gruff voice cried out in pain and something thudded heavily to the ground nearby. Wiping his eyes, the world finally came into soft focus. Coach Teren sat directly before him, holding his forehead. Beside them was an empty plastic cooler that had once been filled with Gatorade.

"Damn! You've got a hard head, kid," Teren moaned.

Cameron could barely make his voice out of the roar that rose and fell around them. A forest of legs belonging to teammates and officials surrounded him. Hands reached down to pat him on the shoulder.

He covered his ears with his hands and tried to roll himself into a ball. The world began to blur out again. The voices around him rose with concern in response.

More hands touched him. The shuffling of the legs grew frantic.

A voice suddenly pierced the din.

"Cam? Cam? Will you people give him some room?" Then, closer to his face. Softer. "Cam?" His mother's voice. He could always smell coffee on her breath, though she never drank it.

Usually, he was comforted by this. This time, he found himself recoiling.

Now her hand was on his shoulder, a delicate, bony claw attempting to soothe him. He attempted to shrug it away.

"It's Mom, dear," and the claw remained on his shoulder.

His eyes focused. She had crouched down, so much smaller than he, so much smaller than the bulky figures around them. She seemed to shrink even smaller as he looked; he thought someone might accidentally step on her. And thought, maybe that would be a good thing.

There was another surge of noise and activity from the crowd. The ambulance had arrived. Paramedics descended upon him and Coach Teren. A stretcher was laid out beside Cameron.

"Get back and let them do their jobs, Geri, for chrissakes!" The sound of Aunt Claudia's voice was a thousand nails on a thousand chalkboards. A cloud of her favorite cologne accompanied her, a scent that reminded Cameron of dying lilacs. She emerged from the crowd, which couldn't part quickly enough to let her pass, stepping quickly but gingerly through the mud of the end zone. She looked like an angry ostrich, her head perched on a thin neck with a large Adam's apple. Huge eyes, and utterly uncaring. With one strong hand she roughly pulled his mother up to her feet. In her other hand she held a metal nail file.

"But Claudia . . ." Her protest withered in a glance from the angry ostrich. His mother turned and disappeared back into the crowd. The ostrich turned back to regard him with those large, black eyes, full of disdain.

He thought of his father. The sound and smell of his father's blood sizzling on his face overwhelmed his senses. The world blurred and then retreated completely.

3

His father revisited him in a loop-tape dream, a sort of highlight reel of his end zone vision. Over and over, his father, vengeance's quarterback; himself, the Amazing Bifurcated Boy! Liberal doses of turtles and lizards, of fire and blood, of Aunt Claudia and his mother, the former riding a broom, the latter sweeping with one as it burned. He saw a flaming lizard that lived in the burned-out shell of a giant turtle. The fiery creature darted from hole to hole unceasingly. The dream would end when his father cried "Vengeance!" and burst into sizzling flame. And then it would begin again. And this *was* a dream, his father's image only a duplicate, an analog recording of the spirit that Cameron had encountered in the end zone.

Finally, Cameron noticed a new element in the dream. A white snowflake, the size of his hand, floating in the sky. It danced above the flames, on thermal drafts, but did not melt. Cameron caught the snowflake in an upturned palm. Its whiteness was almost a glow; it radiated cold. He brought it closer to his face to examine it. It smelled antiseptic, with an underlying sweet, flowery scent.

The nightmare loop started to cue up again. Cameron couldn't take it anymore, so he buried his face in the snowflake.

And fell in.

He woke up then, but didn't open his eyes immediately. Reaching out with his other senses, he assured himself that this indeed was reality and not simply another dream, another trap. But the antiseptic smell was strong now, and of a perfectly ordinary, nonportentous quality. The flowery scent belonged to the living world. So he opened his eyes.

He was in a hospital room, bright, sterile and cold. The color in the room besides the institutional aqua was provided by hordes of potted plants and flowers placed on every available surface around the bed.

Before he could smile, Cameron frowned. Lots of flowers meant he'd been out for longer than overnight. Not a good sign.

Then he caught sight of the action figure holding a spray of hand-picked dandelions on the stand next to him. Cameron plucked the card held in the figure's other hand and read,

> *Uber-Cam!*
> *We did it!*

And the doctor says the cleat-marks on my back will eventually go away.

> *Get well!*
> *Ben Rosenberg,*
> *Pete Gyllenhal*

Cameron smiled to himself as he put the card back in the superhero's well-sculpted hand, then swung his legs out to stand. His stiff muscles protested. He stretched out a little, then stood slowly.

Inspecting the other bunches of flowers and get-well gifts, Cameron found one from his mother and Aunt Claudia. The entire message and signature was in his mother's delicate script. He would have been surprised if Aunt Claudia even knew that card or flowers existed. Next to them were a dozen long-stemmed roses in a vase, no doubt sent by his girlfriend, Sofia. He plucked one rose from the vase and brought it to his nose. Closing his eyes, he let the scent remind him of her—and to overcome the last of the coppery blood smell that seemed to remain from his dream.

A large paper banner reading GET WELL CAM! hung over the entrance to the room. It was signed by the entire football team, including Coach Teren, who added a note in his nearly illegible scrawl: "At least the only goose egg you gave me was on my forehead, ya rat bastard!"

Cameron chuckled and turned to a small potted tree, next to the largest, and by far the most ugly and ostentatious floral arrangement he had ever seen. The bonsai tree was, of course, from his roommate, Harry. The gigantic bouquet, though, was a mystery. If he hadn't already read Rosenberg and Gyllenhal's card on the action figure, he would have thought this tacky creation was one of theirs.

As he lifted the card from its holder, the door opened behind him. Before he could turn around, he heard a squeal of delight and soon had a body wrapped around him from behind.

"Hey!" he cried out and dropped the card.

A flurry of kisses rained upon his neck. He twisted in his attacker's grasp and faced her, countering her kiss for kiss. He could feel her full chest against his, and ran one hand down her long, silky hair to the small of her back. Then he encircled her waist, lifted her up and threw her on the hospital bed, tumbling with her, on top of her.

Minutes later, they had to come up for air.

"Look who's back!" Sofia grinned.

"I had to come back to you," he said.

"Aren't you sweet?" she replied. "I think I'll keep you."

He rolled off her and flipped onto his back, his arm cradling her head. They lay across the short end of the bed, their feet dangling over the edge, legs kicking like two kids fishing at the end of a country dock.

"I saw you looking at the god-awful arrangement," Sofia said after a few moments of silence. She rolled over on her side and propped her head on her hand. Her hair cascaded down, fanning behind her luxuriously. "You know who gave you that?"

Cameron shook his head. "Nope."

"Blake Chesterland."

Cameron thought for a moment, then shrugged. "Don't know him."

"The guy who put you in here, dummy!" She playfully slapped his shoulder. "The asshole who made the late hit."

"Really?"

"Yeah, I found out who he was, called him up and told him you were in the hospital, and that if he didn't show he was sorry for what he'd done, I was going to hunt him down and kick his ass!" Her eyes flared dramatically.

Cameron snorted out a laugh, then all at once curled on his side, his back to her, hysterical.

She started kicking him. "Don't laugh. I'm serious. Bastard knocked you out with a low blow, and of course he didn't even get the penalty because your team declined it!" Her voice was fiercely indignant. "The bastard's gotta pay. Even if I'm the one to make him do it."

His laughter trailing to giggles, he flipped and faced her again. He had to agree, Sofia could probably take this Chesterland character. She was quick, athletic and strong. And fearless.

"Listen to you!" he said. "You're like my personal Ah-nold!"

She shook his head. "No way. Sigourney Weaver all the way." Then she lowered her voice and snarled, "Get away from him, you bitch!"

They both surrendered to a giggle fit this time. And Cameron suddenly realized this was a fine time to tickle her, so he started to gently poke her in the ribs, while she helplessly cried, "Stop!"

Then the door opened and the two quickly stopped and sat up in bed. Sofia took one look at the new guest and growled.

"Knock much, Larry?" she yelled at her brother. "Get out of here!"

Cameron patted her on the leg. "Come on. You've got to learn to be nicer." Then he turned to Larry, who stood dumbly in the doorway, one hand on the doorknob and the other fidgeting with the strap on the backpack he was never seen without.

He and Sofia were fraternal twins, so different that they didn't even seem to be the same species, let alone from the same family. Where Sofia was athletic, graceful and lithe, her brother was a beanbag chair with a head and legs. Sofia was the epitome of style while Larry's fashions were a timeless mélange of mismatched rumple. Plain and simple, Larry was slow, and whether this was just an appropriate adjective or indicated a physiological or psychological condition, no one was quite sure. Dr. Paulsen just said that Larry was lazy.

Despite their father's constant battles with his

daughter, and perhaps because of them, Sofia got a lion's share of the attention in the family. As for Larry, Dr. Paulsen openly regarded him as a disappointment. Sadly, this did nothing to diminish Larry's desire for his father's affection. He worshiped his father, but Dr. Paulsen either couldn't tell or didn't care. Once, Larry had asked Cameron to marry Sofia, and take her away so that their dad would pay more attention to him. The confidence had broken his heart—he never told Sofia what her brother had said—and spurred him to act the older brother whenever possible.

"Hi, Cameron." Larry's monotone voice was so nasal, one would expect his nostrils to have lips. "If you're better, then you wanna play a quick two-out-of-three of Rock-Paper-Scissors?"

Cameron was about to agree to their little ritual when Sofia cut in. "Didn't Dad say we had to go, Larry?"

"Come on honey, we have time for a quick game." He winked at her.

"Oh, Cameron," Sofia said, rolling over on her stomach to show how put-upon she was right now.

Larry approached the bed, his expression rippling between hopeful and worried. Rock-Paper-Scissors was a ritual he and Cameron had begun two years ago. Too slow mentally or physically for most games or sports, it was the only contest in which he could participate as a worthy opponent. Even more important to Larry, no one could take advantage of him;

there was no way to cheat. The game was too immediate for that. But Larry had never beaten Cameron, and his enjoyment had lately become an obsession. Playing double or nothing for two years, Larry had racked up a debt of $20 million. Though neither of them considered it an actual debt, canceling it out fair and square became a matter of pride for Larry. He had even begun to develop anxiety attacks over it. When Cameron offered to stop playing, this only served to upset Larry more. So Cameron always indulged his friend.

"Okay, I'll count first," Larry said, putting his hands behind his back.

"You got it." Cameron did the same.

"One, two, three," Larry counted. On three, both held out their hands. Larry's fist was in a ball. Cameron's fingers were splayed out. He put his hand over Larry's fist.

"Paper smothers rock!" Cameron announced.

Larry's breath hitched just a bit, but then he nodded. "Okay, second one, I'll count it." He did, and on three, they put out their hands again.

Larry wiggled his two fingers at Cameron's splayed hand. "Scissors cuts paper!" he shouted as if he had just hit a home run.

"Okay Larry, my turn," Cameron said. He shot a sly glance at Sofia, who just rolled her eyes at him and tried very hard to act disinterested.

"One, two, *three!*" And out came their hands.

Larry had scissors. Cameron played rock. He mock-bashed Larry's hand.

"Rock breaks scissors, buddy. You owe me . . ." he pretended to do a complex calculation in his head. "Forty million dollars!"

Larry pinched his mouth closed. He appeared ready to hyperventilate, but a grunt at the doorway distracted him.

"Mmmmm . . . Larry," came a voice almost as dull as Larry's. "I told you to hurry it up."

Larry swiveled around, forgetting his frustration. Dr. Paul Paulsen filled the width of the door, if not the height. He was dressed, as always, like a mortician. On his tie was an ugly gold clip, like golden goose droppings splattered on his chest. No suit worn by the man was complete without it.

Dr. Paulsen frowned at Larry. Then he laid eyes on Cameron and the expression darkened further.

"Mmmmm . . . Ah, Cameron," he said, stepping into the room. Larry scuttled out of the way.

"Dr. P.," Cameron replied.

Dr. Paulsen wrinkled his nose slightly. He hated that nickname. Ignoring Cameron, he turned to his daughter. "Mmmmm . . . Time to go, Sofia. Now."

"Okay, *Dad*," Sofia rolled her eyes. "But one more minute."

Dr. Paulsen grunted in reply and turned. Larry had settled in the doorway. The older man grunted again and it finally dawned on Larry to move out of his father's way. He stepped aside and his father marched out. Larry continued to stand there for a moment, seeming lost, until Dr. Paulsen grunted, "MMmmmm . . . Larry!" Like shaking himself out of a dream, Larry snapped to attention, turned and left the room.

Sofia flopped herself back onto the bed.

"Stupid mechanic! I want my car back!"

"Most people *like* traveling with an entourage," Cameron teased.

"Ugh. Some entourage. More like a freak show. Just so you know, my dad is using this as yet another example of why you're no good for me."

Cameron sat on a chair opposite the bed. "Why this time?"

"Because," Sofia said, sitting up, "if you get injured in real sports, you'll either be ruined with no 'marketable'—his word—skills, or you'll die and leave me a widow. Or worse, you'll be a hopeless vegetable and I'll have to give up my life to take care of you. In any event, this is the new way you could ruin my life."

"Wow. He really thought that through."

"Except that he's imagining me as some football wife, sitting in the bleachers, hosting luncheons, crap like that." She shuddered in disgust. "Sorry, honey, I'll catch your games on the tube, but I'll be very busy with my career as an eminent psychologist."

"Oh, just like Dad!"

Sofia shook her head emphatically. "No, Dad's a

guidance counselor. I'm going to be a real doctor. And really help people."

A face appeared in the small, square window set in the door. Dr. Paulsen frowned through it. And grunted. Then disappeared.

"Looks like the bus is leaving," Cameron told her.

Sofia rose unwillingly. "Get out of here, okay?"

"Probably tonight. I have to call my mom. And I should probably tell the hospital that I'm up and around."

He kissed her, repeatedly, until another muffled grunt at the tiny window stopped them, and she left.

4

The hospital discharged Cameron a few hours later. He declined an invitation—a plea, really—to be taken home by his mother. It would have meant having to face Aunt Claudia, which even in the best of circumstances was undesirable. Now, Cameron didn't know how he'd react to her. He wasn't even sure if he *should* react any differently to her. While he distinguished his rapid-fire dreams from his end zone vision, that still didn't mean his father had visited him. Or that Aunt Claudia had murdered his father.

"Well, considering how you feel about your aunt Claudia, I could see your mind making something like that up," said Harry.

His roommate had picked Cameron up in his battered blue pickup. In the back, the numerous gift plants shed leaves and petals at each bump. He had listened as Cameron spoke, at first falteringly, then, as if caught in a spell, more passionately about his experiences in the last few days.

"You sound like Sofia," Cameron replied.

"Oh, is that what she said?"

Cameron shook his head steadily. "No way. I haven't told her."

"Why not?"

"Because she'll worry about me, whether it's true or not. And if it *is* true, I don't want to involve her in what I might have to do."

Harry made a too-quick stop at a stoplight and then jetted into the intersection. Several plants fell over in the back.

"And what would you have to do?" Harry asked.

Cameron thought for a moment. "Get revenge. Like Dad asked."

"What would that entail?" Harry didn't like the sound of this at all. "Besides, how could she have killed him? He had a heart attack."

"My father was healthy as an ox, you know that."

"They ran in your family, according to your aunt Claudia."

"Yeah, how convenient for her," Cameron said darkly.

Cameron thought back to the look on his father's face, the silent scream, the hand clutched to his chest. A smudge of blood on his shirt seeping from a triangular cut on his finger.

"It's her fault anyway," he said suddenly. "She gave him the turtle in the first place."

"What, you think the turtle was poisonous?" He laughed. Cameron slumped down in his seat.

"I already checked. There *are* no poisonous turtles. Besides, this one was a normal old painted turtle, very, very common." His mind went back to his father's cut. "But for a turtle, ornery as hell. Bit him all the time, but he treated it like a dog or a cat. This time when it bit him, he seized up or something."

"I've heard of that," Harry said. "Like how suddenly pricking your finger can cause a heart attack, or riding on a roller coaster can cause an aneurysm. Or those athletes who just drop dead on the court or field. It's usually some preexisting condition that gets triggered by some stressful event."

"Yeah, yeah." Cameron didn't want to hear rational things that made sense. He wanted proof that his father had returned to him, if only briefly and if only in a vision. "The thing that burns me up is that Aunt Claudia was more upset about the turtle dying than my father. Cremated the damn thing."

The image of the turtle in flames danced in his head. Cameron straightened in his seat. A sense of déjà vu coursed through him, like momentary dizziness.

"Leave it to a herpetologist," Harry laughed. "No wonder your aunt Claudia is so messed up. Not only does she relate to animals better than people, but the animals she relates to aren't known for their expressiveness or shows of affection. Unless you count being squeezed to death by a boa constrictor a hug." Harry shook his head in amusement as he pulled into their parking spot.

Cameron didn't notice. He had turned his thoughts inward. In the darkness of his mind, he saw something glittering and red in the distance. He reached for it. But it eluded his grasp.

Wordlessly, he slipped out of the car and started up to the apartment he and Harry shared.

"Hey!" Harry called after him. "What about your stuff?"

"I'm beat," Cameron said, only half paying attention. "I'll come out after dinner."

"Okeydoke. I'll grab a couple on my way up," Harry said as he headed to the back of the truck.

When Cameron got to his room, he couldn't sleep. The harder he reached for the glimmering speck in his mind, the farther it stayed out of his reach. So he switched on his computer, fired up the DSL, and roamed the world from his bedroom. By the time he had finished, eyes drooping and watery, the cold glow from his monitor the only light in the room, he had proven to himself that the Internet was good for something besides porn after all.

Stumbling from his room, he found that while he was jacked in, Harry had brought up all his flowers and plants. Harry had even tacked the banner up over the shabby card table set up in the dining room.

"Harry!" he called out. In his hands, he held a stack of paper he had printed out during his online investigation.

"Coming," Harry called out. He emerged from his room on the opposite side of the apartment in shorts and a T-shirt, dirty white socks on his feet, one half-off, flopping before him. He held a cordless phone to his ear. He mouthed "It's Shayne," to Cameron, who sat at the dining-room table and spread out his research.

"Hey, hon, Cameron's up. Can I call ya back?" He paused for the reply. Cameron could hear a rhythmic buzzing, like the speech of an adult in a Charlie Brown TV special. "Okay, love you too," Harry said when the buzzing stopped and clicked off the phone.

"What up?" he asked, approaching the table.

"I thought you were going out with Shayne tonight," Cameron said.

"Yeah, well, she wasn't feeling good and I wanted to stick around in case you needed anything, so it's all right." Harry sat across the table from Cameron with a decisive flop to his left sock. "So let's see." And he started pulling papers from across the table and rotating them so he could read.

"Hmmm," he said. They showed various reptiles, mostly snakes and lizards. "Death adder, very nice," Harry commented. "Ah, my personal favorite, king cobra." He held up one picture of a bulbous-looking lizard, with a tail as wide and flat as its head, and bumpy skin like it was a child's art project. The picture wasn't labeled.

"Who's this fine fellow?" Harry asked. "Gila monster?"

"Mexican beaded lizard," Cameron answered.

"Taking a sudden interest in your aunt's vocation?" Harry said. "Looking to follow in her scaly-toed footsteps?" He was teasing, but Cameron's eyes remained deadly serious.

"Look, this is going to sound crazy," Cameron began.

"I can't wait," Harry said and made himself comfortable. He stretched back on his chair and crossed his left leg over his right, flopping his sock as he did so. "Hit me."

"So we know that turtles aren't poisonous, right?"

Harry nodded. They had confirmed that one on the way back from the hospital.

"And lots and lots of snakes *are* poisonous."

Harry nodded again. "Aside from their general appearance, it's what makes them so popular for scary stories and movies and stuff. It's why Indiana Jones didn't ask the musical question, 'Turtles, why did it have to be turtles?' "

Cameron should have laughed at this one too, but he didn't. In fact, he looked hurt, almost horrified. Harry took note and sat up again, focusing on his friend's intense look.

"There are only two poisonous lizards in the whole world. One is the Gila monster, which is native to the

U.S., and the other is its cousin, native of Mexico and north Central America." Cameron pointed to each of these creatures, represented on the printouts between them.

"Almost any of these, particularly the snakes, contain poison that, in higher or lower doses can simulate the effects of a heart attack."

Harry leaned forward and eyed his friend suspiciously. He glanced down at the pictures.

"You're not saying your aunt poisoned your dad, are you?"

Harry was a smart guy, and Cameron knew that his friend could see what he had seen earlier, the shimmering red idea in the distance.

"Yes. And no." Harry regarded him thoughtfully. There was a certain skepticism in his expression, but that didn't bother Cameron. He knew his friend would at least listen.

He revealed the glimmering red idea to Harry.

"She killed him with the turtle."

Harry didn't speak at first. Instead, he crossed his arms, flopped his sock and turned the shiny red object over in his mind.

"But turtles aren't poisonous," he said slowly, aware he was stating the obvious, and that Cameron must have a response to that.

"Exactly, which is why no one would think poison, especially not from a painted turtle." He paused. Harry had no comment, so he went on. "And it wasn't a snake or snake poison—a snakebite would be ultra obvious, even at the scene. And he didn't have a bourbon or brandy or any of the things people typically put poison in in murder mysteries."

Harry remained silent, continuing to absorb the information. His left foot started jittering, causing the sock to dance around beneath the table.

"Okay, so you take a poison—distilled, concentrated, natural strength, I don't know—and you put it in the turtle, in its mouth. Okay, so you have a delivery system no one would expect. And you don't use death adder poison or cobra poison, because they're probably hard to procure, even for a noted herpetologist like my aunt Claudia. The fact that those kinds of snakes are rare here would make their poison, and especially a bite mark, pretty conspicuous. So what you do, if you have the perfect delivery system—a turtle known to bite the hand that feeds it—is you find a poison that is both effective, readily available and unlikely to attract attention: beaded lizard or Gila monster poison."

"Wow." It was the only word Harry spoke for several minutes. He just stared down and contemplated his floppy sock, which he twitched left and right as he thought.

"And your proof is?" Harry finally asked, dubious.

"Gone, of course. The turtle's been cremated. And who knows if the poison would show up this long after my dad's death." Harry had leaned back in his chair again. His expression looked disturbingly like he was studying a very strange, and potentially dangerous, insect. Cameron pounded on the table. "I know that's how it went down, Harry! I know it! I dreamed it! Whether I saw my dad's ghost or not . . . Who knows? Maybe I picked up some psychic vibration. But I dreamed the turtle and I dreamed the lizard. That's how I know she didn't use snake venom."

"Cuz you dreamed it," Harry repeated, almost wincing.

"Dammit, Harry!" Cameron stood suddenly, sweeping the papers from the tabletop. His chair fell over behind him with a thump. "Aunt Claudia killed my father! And she's not going to get away with it!"

"Okay bro, calm down." Harry spoke evenly. "But listen. Let's say that's true. Your logic, twisted though it is, makes sense to me. It does. But you've described the perfect crime—no witnesses, no clues, the murder weapon cremated—what can you do?"

Cameron righted his chair and sat down on it again. He leaned forward, templing his fingers and balancing his chin on the steeple.

"I've been thinking of that too," he said. *"The Tell-Tale Heart."*

"The Edgar Allan Poe story?"

"Yep."

Harry fell back to contemplating his sock when the phone rang.

"Cameron, honey?" said the voice. "It's Mom."

"Hey, Mom."

Harry looked up sharply.

"Are you standing, dear?" she asked, her voice sounding strange. From behind, he could hear Aunt Claudia's voice.

"For chrissakes, Geri, just say it!"

"I'm sitting, Mom," he said quickly, but he continued to stand.

"There's good news and bad news, darling." In the background, Claudia roared in frustration. "The bad news is that there's been another death in the family." Then she quickly added, "But it's no one you know, so don't worry about that."

"Is that the good news?" he asked.

"No, that's not the good news," she said.

His mother wasn't selling the tragedy of a death in her tone, so he didn't panic. But a tremble in her voice hinted at some sort of excitement.

"Then what's the good news?"

5

"I've inherited a castle?" asked Cameron.

A moment ago, when the lawyer rasped across the mahogany desk in his lifetime smoker's voice that he had inherited nearly four billion dollars from a previously unknown relative, the statement had barely registered. To his left, his mother had gasped and slumped in her seat. To his right, Claudia had made no noise, but her body had gone instantly rigid. Cameron was so far from being able to connect with the reality of the statement, that he could only frown. The old cigar-smoke odor of the room simply intensified. Then the lawyer, whose appearance matched the antique atmosphere of the office, had mentioned a castle.

"A famous landmark, actually," replied the lawyer, whose desk placard identified him as Eldred R. Murray, Esquire. "The seat of power for many kings of Denmark, from which you are descended." He could have been delivering news that Cameron's shirts were ready at the dry cleaner's.

"I'm, like, royal?" Cameron asked, his voice an astonished squeak.

This finally brought a smile to Eldred R. Murray, Esquire's face. "Like, yes."

The enormity of the situation finally penetrated Cameron's skull. Like a railroad spike to the forehead. Once again, consciousness threatened to declare itself optional when Claudia's voice cut through the cigar-smoke haze about to envelop Cameron.

"This money. Where does it come from?" Her tone was both demanding and desperate. She fidgeted desperately, obsessively filing her nails, then pocketing the file, then bringing it back out again when she just couldn't keep still.

Papers shuffled on the desk. "Old money, king's treasure and all that, numerous landholdings, investments," said Eldred R. Murray, Esquire. "And such."

"And why . . . him?" Claudia snorted.

"Now Claudia . . ." began Geri.

"He's a boy!"

"Hey! I'll be twenty-one, soon!" Cameron protested.

"A *boy* who's never met this man. I'm a nearer blood relative."

Eldred shuffled more papers on his desk, looked down at them and cleared his throat. "Young Cameron here is the nearest living *male* relative, however. The will is quite clear that as long as there are male heirs, the legacy can only be passed down to them."

"That's sexist!" Claudia was seething.

"Perhaps." The lawyer settled back in his chair and tapped his fingertips together absently. "But not illegal."

Cameron leaned across the desk toward the lawyer, as if sharing a confidence. He whispered, but very loudly, "She's worried I'm not going to give her an allowance."

"Cameron!" His mother rose from her swoon to scold him.

"Sorry," he said immediately, and insincerely. But Cameron was enjoying this. The money, the castle, the new family history—he saw his opportunity to finally lord it over his father's evil sister.

Eldred R. Murray's large, wet eyes finally seemed focused on the proceedings. Families squabbling over inheritances always amused him. Any doubt his amusement was not intentional or perverse was dispelled in his next statement.

"Of course," he rasped. "The inheritance must be held in trust until that time."

This caused the evil smile on Cameron's face to wilt. It instantly bloomed across Claudia's.

"Who, then, manages the inheritance until that time?" she asked.

"His legal guardians. His parents. You two."

Cameron settled back in his seat with a grunt. Geri instantly laid a hand on his knee to soothe him.

"It's only for a month or so, hon," she cooed.

He looked straight into his aunt's eyes. "I could be dead by then."

"Cameron!" his mother gasped. "What a horrible—" and could say no more.

Claudia turned on Cameron and stared daggers at him, but did not speak. Cameron didn't look away. He searched her eyes for a red glimmer, for a sign that his comment would dredge up something inside his aunt. The ostrich eyes looked more angry than usual, but they betrayed little else.

If tension were blood, then Eldred R. Murray, Esquire, was a vampire easing himself into a bubble bloodbath as he settled back into his great leather chair. A barely audible squeal of delight escaped his lips as the family before him jockeyed for position. They always did at the reading of a will.

Slowly, Claudia went back to filing her nails, still regarding Cameron with unadulterated hate.

Cameron himself broke the tension by looking away and clearing his throat. He realized that this inheritance put a new spin on his plot to break Aunt Claudia down and make her admit to killing his father. If he could bide his time, the money and resources at his disposal could open up new opportunities to deal with his aunt. Just knowing he possessed such wealth would itself drive her half crazy. He'd hardly have to lift a finger except to sign some documents. *As they say,* he thought, *success is the best revenge. So let's rub it in,* was the next thought that passed through his mind. Cameron turned abruptly to Eldred R. Murray, Esquire.

"So this castle. When can we see it?"

"What? Oh." Eldred creaked forward in his chair, surprised to be pulled back into the conversation so quickly. They usually spent more time going for each other's throats. He shuffled more papers, more to shift gears in his mind than because he needed any information contained in them.

"Immediately, if you wish." He shrugged. "Its maintenance is provided for, in perpetuity, so there's nothing you need worry about."

"But if I had a passport and a plane ticket?"

"It would be prepared for you to live in, whatever you like, within two weeks. Certainly."

"Excellent." An idea had formed in Cameron's mind. It wouldn't solve all of his problems, if any, but it would be fun and Aunt Claudia would hate it. "In that case, make it so."

"If you wish," replied Eldred R. Murray, Esquire, with a shrug.

"But *we* don't wish." Claudia nearly pounded the desktop.

"Aw, come on," Cameron pleaded, injecting an entirely false note of whininess into his voice. "I want to celebrate my birthday there."

"That sounds like a nice idea," said Geri. "You mean all of us, don't you, dear? After all that's happened, we could all use a vacation."

"Well yes, but—" began Claudia, but Cameron had momentum and pressed on.

"Yeah, all of us. But I don't want this to be some stuffy family birthday party. It's gotta be a blowout. The blowout to end all blowouts! So I want to bring Sofia and all the guys in the football team. It'll rage!"

"Honey, most of those kids couldn't afford it."

"Of course not, Mom. But I could."

Claudia's head suddenly went whipping from side to side. She pointed the nail file at him. "No way. Forget it. Do you know what kind of money that would cost?"

Cameron pointed to himself. "Excuse me. Rich guy, here."

"In a month," Claudia snapped back. "I'm not going to let you waste that money on your stupid friends."

"It's bad form to throw money around like that, Cameron," added Geri.

Cameron didn't even blink. He turned to his unwitting ally, Eldred R. Murray, Esquire. "I know you're a lawyer and not an accountant, but tell me, if I were gonna pay the airfare for, say, one hundred people or so to Denmark, how much of a month's worth of interest on this inheritance would it take? Ballpark."

"Coach, business or first class?"

"Coach. Fourteen-day advance ticket purchase. No need to be ostentatious." He winked at his mother.

"No indeed," replied Eldred. He ran the numbers through his head. He smiled when he came up with the answer. He could practically taste the conflict between the boy and his aunt.

"Frankly, that wouldn't even put a dent in a day's worth of interest income."

Cameron turned to his mother and Claudia.

"See?"

"No. I won't have it. Light cigars with hundred dollar bills *after* your birthday." Claudia wanted to add, *If you live that long*, but only barely restrained herself. "But until then, you're not getting more than an allowance from me. And you can fund an army to invade Denmark on the allowance I have in mind."

"Mom!"

Geri was silent for a moment. Her face showed obvious conflict. There was a moment when he thought she would buckle. Suddenly, a backbone grew where one existed all too infrequently. Cameron's mother laid a spidery hand on Claudia's.

"Now, Claudia. This is an extraordinary situation. Extraordinarily positive in light of all the bad things that have gone on. Cameron deserves to celebrate his birthday, with his friends, in *his* castle."

"But Geri—"

"Now don't interrupt me this time, Claudia."

When she decided to be, Geri could be irresistible, a trait Cameron's father adored. The memories, of his father alive, of his mother as she used to be, made Cameron a bit sad.

"One little splurge, relative to the amount of money we're talking about, isn't going to hurt." It had been a long time since she had taken Cameron's side against Claudia, and didn't budge. "And both of us know that Cameron isn't the sort to let something like this go to his head and get out of control."

Enclosing Claudia's hand in hers, she took Cameron's hand with her free one.

"You two don't get along. Never did. But we're family, and I love you both. And perhaps this is just the thing to heal our wounds and bring us together."

Stupid bitch, thought Eldred R. Murray, Esquire. Couldn't she be conciliatory and diplomatic somewhere else? His lips trembled briefly, but otherwise, his face never let go of his expression of witless warmth.

Geri turned first to Cameron, then to Claudia.

"We're going to Denmark to celebrate Cameron's birthday. With *all* his friends."

Claudia's granite crumbled, and she squeezed Geri's hand.

"All right. These last few months have been rough on all of us." She sighed and turned to Eldred R. Murray, Esquire, Estate Lawyer. "All right. We agree. Let's do it." She turned back to Geri and smiled, a smile that appeared like a seismic fissure in her face and then disappeared.

Shortly after, they all rose, thanked the lawyer and departed.

* * *

The car ride home was spent in what seemed to be stunned silence over the news. In reality, Cameron was thinking how he and Harry might modify their Tell-Tale Heart plan based on what would be essentially unlimited resources. Geri drove, mostly keeping her eyes on the road, and being careful not to say anything that would anger Claudia and cause another spat. But it would have been hard to break Claudia out of her reverie. Her mind was already working on ways to ensure that Cameron wouldn't come within a mile of that money.

6

Over the coming weeks, Cameron and his mother made arrangements while Claudia simply oversaw the accounting. To Cameron's surprise, his aunt was relatively cooperative, but just cranky enough for him not to be overly suspicious of her. He soon became so embroiled in plans for the trip that lizards, turtles, poison, murder, vengeance and even thoughts of his father faded to the background. When they did cross his mind, he simply vowed to readdress the issue when his inheritance was settled, the day he turned twenty-one and would officially control his own fortune.

During this period, time took on a maddeningly erratic quality for those involved in the trip. For some, the seconds could not tick by fast enough. Others wished that, by removing the batteries from their watches, time would actually stop. So much to do, so little time to prepare for a trip that, conversely, couldn't begin quickly enough.

The announcement of the party stunned the campus. Cameron's popularity, always high among the student population, reached phenomenal proportions. Anyone who had been on the fence about Cameron, or who had reason to dislike him, did a rapid about-face, figuring anyone worth a few billion dollars couldn't be all bad.

Those invited to the birthday bash in Denmark benefited from a disproportional rise in their own popularity. Fierce competition erupted among those wishing to accompany the few single football players on the trip. Relationships were destroyed as non-football players lost girlfriends who suddenly set their sights on another guy. Female students faced off against their best friends or even sisters. Pierson told Cameron that one girl had sent him a photograph of her modeling a very skimpy bikini. Unbeknownst to her, the girl's boyfriend had already sent him a PlayStation 2. Ultimately, Pierson gave his ticket to the winner of a local sorority's wet T-shirt and lap dance contest. The wet T-shirt contest had been the sorority's idea; the lap dance component had been Pierson's.

Only Rosenberg and Gyllenhal escaped the feeding frenzy unscathed. Their efforts included a full-page ad in the school newspaper (for which they both worked), flyers around campus and even setting up a "kissing booth" near the student union. Their only customer was a ten-year-old girl who had been visiting a relative. She had mistaken the booth for a lemonade stand and left threatening to tell her mommy on them for trying to trick little kids. The boys greeted this with their customary good humor and unparalleled skills of rationalization. In the end, they gave up trying and decided just to do what they always did, hang with each other.

When the smoke cleared, everyone finally found themselves at the airport, waiting to board the plane. They were nervous and excited. Cameron was just exhausted. The highlight reel of the end zone vision had returned a week before. So, he and Harry had gone out and bought provisions for the trip. The dream left heavy rotation just after, which provided some relief, but his emotions had been stirred up and he felt haunted again. He had bought an additional item, something that Harry didn't know about, and it made him feel just a little better.

At the airport, when he was certain that his mother, Claudia and Dr. Paulsen were occupied, he sneaked off to pay in advance for all the alcohol on the flight. Even though his money was currently in trust, he had some access, and intended to squeeze out as much as he could to make this trip a success. He knew his friends would appreciate a steady, free supply of alcohol. When he returned, mission accomplished, he found Sofia huddled with Shayne and several other girls near the gate. She waved him over. As he approached, he saw several unfamiliar faces. When he joined the group, he slipped an arm around Sofia and gave her a quick kiss.

"Plotting, are you?" he asked.

He searched the gate area for Harry. He spotted

him quickly, about twenty feet away, tall and lanky, tapping his foot absently while he talked to Rosenberg and Gyllenhal. Their eyes met and Harry winked at him conspiratorially. Cameron winked back.

"No plotting," Sofia told him. "Just girl talk."

Cameron did his manly duty and wrinkled his nose at the phrase, "girl talk." As usual, Sofia was playing den mother. He could tell she would be a great group counselor when she got her license to practice.

"Everybody excited?" he asked. Heads bobbed up and down.

"Yeah, Cammy," said Atara, a shapely, voluptuous African-American cheerleader. "You are *so* sweet to share your good fortune with us all. My Ty-baby wanted me to come thank you for the both of us." Her "Ty-baby" was Ty Warrington, the team's field goal kicker. He professed to hate that nickname, but behind the scenes (and Sofia had told him this in strictest confidence), he got *way* turned-on whenever Atara whispered it in his ear. She stepped forward to kiss Cameron noisily on the cheek.

"Umm . . . and you taste sweet, too, baby," she purred afterward.

He blushed. "Aw shucks, ma'am."

"Hey Cam!" Eric suddenly appeared, his hands on the shoulders of a small, dark-haired girl Cameron did not recognize. His teammate towered over the girl. "Have you met Kay?"

"No, not yet," Cameron replied, and stepped forward to shake her hand. As he did, Eric turned his head ever so slightly and glanced at Shayne, who was also looking at him. The two exchanged a poison glance and turned away from each other. The exchange lasted half a second, and was only barely noticeable. But Cameron had noticed.

Then the girl's thin, pale hand was in his, shaking it.

"Aloo," she said. "I am Kay." She bobbed her head quickly in greeting, her short hair snapping perfectly forward and back. She wore the overly bright smile of someone new to America and not fluent in English. "Thank you, Cameron." His name came out *Cam-urrrr-own.*

He shook her hand politely. "You are very welcome, Kay."

He cocked his head curiously at Eric, who was smiling blithely, apparently not aware that his silent exchange with Shayne had been witnessed.

"She's Danish, from Copenhagen. A foreign exchange student at Globe."

"I am happy to go home," Kay said, head bobbing again, hair whipping perfectly as if elastic. "My brother is sick and I need to go quickly."

"How did you two meet?"

In response, Eric put his hand over Kay's on the armrest between them. They exchanged a loving glance as if preparing to announce their engagement.

"eBay," Kay chirped.

"Excuse me?" asked Cameron. This was worthy of a triple take. "You auctioned the trip?"

Eric looked a little sheepish. "I'm a little light on funds, Cam. And you know, Kay's brother is sick."

Cameron let him off the hook with a grin and told Kay very sincerely, "I'm sorry about your brother. But I'm glad this will work out for you."

Just then, the airline announced boarding for the flight. Everyone joined their respective dates and a half hour later, the plane rose above the first layer of cloud cover and the journey officially began.

"Hey you're quiet." Sofia grabbed him by the arm and tugged him out of the drowsiness that had been encroaching for the last hour.

"Just thinking," he replied, not turning his head, barely even focusing his eyes.

He and Sofia sat side by side in the extra wide seats of first class. He had easily talked Claudia into upgrade for his family and Sofia. Claudia wouldn't have traveled any other way. Dr. Paul Paulsen sat two rows before them. Officially, he had accompanied the group as an additional chaperone, but everyone knew Dr. P.'s real purpose was to keep close watch over Sofia.

"Ouch!" Sofia had pinched his arm. Hard.

"When I say, 'You're being quiet,' that's your sign to stop being so quiet!" Her arms were folded in an "I-dare-you-to-mess-with-me" gesture.

"Hey, I was almost asleep." Unbuckling his seat

belt, he stood up. "And now I have to hit the head. Be right back."

Cameron headed toward the back of the plane. When he emerged through the curtains separating first class from coach, a cheer rose up in the cabin.

With nearly one hundred of his closest friends, acquaintances and the complete strangers that came with them, the atmosphere resembled a frat party. The free booze had been a good call. Four hours into the flight and already many of his teammates were hammered.

"Hey, it's Cameron!" Pierson shouted, face glowing red from imminent alcohol poisoning. "Woofwoofwoofwoof—" he began and soon the entire Globe contingent of the plane was chanting with him.

Babies cried. The other passengers were clearly unnerved by the rowdy group.

Eric, who was near the bulkhead, jumped to his feet shakily and pumped Cameron's hand.

"Dude, this so totally rocks."

"Enjoying the free cocktails, are ya?" Cameron grinned.

"Dude, you don't know the half of it." Then he looked around furtively. "Check it out." He opened one of two visibly bulging pockets on his cargo pants, revealing a large stash of tiny vodka bottles.

"The flight attendant keeps giving me extra."

"Very cool."

Eric's head bobbed up and down. "Very cool indeed!"

Up ahead sat Marc and Bernie flanked by their respective dates. Marc and Carla were quite a pair. He could have easily filled a second seat; Carla barely filled half of hers. Marc was obviously drunk and trying to talk to Carla. She would periodically say "Uh huh," but her attention was glued to the movie playing on the tiny monitor before her.

Next to them, Bernie was offering a tiny bottle of vodka to Maddy, his pretty blond date. She wrinkled her nose in irritation at him, then returned to the book she was trying very hard to read. Cameron figured she had brought the book as an excuse not to talk to Bernie. Maddy was a freshman Bernie had relentlessly pursued since he laid eyes on her at class registration. She rebuffed him at every turn—until the trip was announced. Even then she played hard to get, presumably weighing the benefits of a trip to Denmark with the downside of traveling with someone she considered a loser.

Cameron caught his teammates' eyes and they saluted him with chess-piece-sized bottles of liquor. He had long since forgiven them for their behavior at the game. After all, Cameron won the game. And his father had been in the end zone, as they warned. Cameron never told them of his experience; they hadn't spoken about it since. Their presence was both proof that something strange had happened to him, and a constant reminder of the event, the sight of them as unsettling as the fiery dreams.

He nodded, acknowledging their toast and continued up the aisle. Hands shot out of rows for high fives as he proceeded. From the back of the plane, he looked like a priest performing a benediction.

Suddenly, Cameron was yanked off his feet. He found himself lying across two passengers' laps.

"Oh, dude, sorry, Cam."

A watery-eyed Pierson had overdone his high five. A large-breasted girl giggled as Pierson pushed Cameron back into the aisle. Pierson introduced her.

"This is Candi," he said. But because of his apparent alcohol intake, it came out, "Thish-iss-Candeeeeee." He belched and added, "She's a tri-delt!"

Ah, the wet T-shirt and lap dance contest winner, he thought, examining her chest and vacant doe eyes. Out loud, he smiled his winning smile and simply said, "Good to have you here. Have fun."

Cameron checked in on Rosenberg and Gyllenhal a few rows back.

"Hey, Cam!" Rosenberg in the aisle seat raised his hand for a high five. Just as Cameron was about to slap him one, Gyllenhal poked his friend in the armpit. Rosenberg gasped and cringed; Gyllenhal stole the first high five.

"Ow." Rosenberg rubbed his chest near his armpit. "That hurt, Pete."

"Don't be such a wuss," Gyllenhal replied. Then he leaned forward across Rosenberg and spoke excitedly to Cameron. "So how's first class? We tried to get up there earlier to say hi, but the flight attendants kicked us out. How's the food? Ow!" Rosenberg abruptly pushed Gyllenhal back into his seat. Then he spoke to Cameron in an excited whisper.

"Is there anyone famous up there?" He then exchanged a hungry look with his friend. "Are flight attendants hotter up there?"

Cameron just laughed. "Actually, yeah. And their uniforms are thongs!"

The freshmen's eyes grew to the size of full moons before they realized that Cameron was kidding them.

"Oh, yeah. Ha! We wish!" Both laughed nervously, embarrassed to have been fooled. Rosenberg moved on quickly.

"Seriously, tho, Cam. Do you get to watch different movies up there?" Gyllenhal asked.

Cameron shrugged. "I don't know. I've just been hanging with Sofia."

"Sofia . . ." both boys murmured under their breath. Then Gyllenhal remembered he had just asked a question.

" 'Cuz some of the other guys were talking about something called the Mile High Club. Everyone seems to think it's the total shit, but it's not in our entertainment guides."

"Is it a sequel to the *First Wives' Club?*" Rosenberg asked innocently.

While Cameron choked on a reply to that, a disturbance rose at the back of the plane. Near the aft toilets, a flight attendant was arguing with a passenger. The buzz-saw whine belonged undoubtedly to Larry.

"Um. I think Mile High Club is playing on the way back," he said quickly. "Catch you later. I gotta see what's going on back there."

". . . my tray is crooked and I can't set down my drink!" Larry was whining as Cameron approached. The smell from the lavatories was distinct.

"Sir," said the beleaguered flight attendant, a prim guy with immobile hair, "You can use the tray next to you, since the seat is vacant."

"But I get cramps in my arm reaching that way! Hey, Cam!" But this was a cry for help, not the appreciative salute of the others on the plane. The prim attendant's head snapped crisply in Cameron's direction. By the look on his face, this had not been the attendant's first encounter with Larry, who had been bumped from first class due to overbooking.

"What's up, Lar?" Cameron asked.

"I can't recline, my entertainment system is screwed up, it smells like crap back here and my tray broke so I can't set down drinks without spilling them on me."

Indeed, Cameron noticed a large pink wet spot from a suicidal glass of red wine on Larry's shirt and lap.

"Can't you move?" he asked, then turned to the attendant. "Can't he switch seats?"

"We have a very full flight this evening, sir. The only empty seat is the one beside the passenger." A bead of sweat rolled from the attendant's perfectly trimmed temple.

"My back hurts, Cam," Larry whined. To emphasize the point, he clutched the small of his back. Leaning forward to do so, he struck his forehead on the seat in front of him.

"Hey!" A woman snarled. "Can you please keep it down? I'm trying to sleep here."

Cameron lowered his voice. "Tell you what, Larry. I'm gonna find someone to swap seats with you, so just sit tight."

"But sir—" began the attendant.

"You can come help me, right?" Cameron said, cutting him off. Seeing his chance to escape, the attendant immediately agreed.

"Gimme a few minutes, Lar." Larry growled, but said he'd hang loose.

Cameron led the prim flight attendant away, fully intending to ask someone to swap with Larry for the remainder of the trip. Another aisle full of high fives, and a few shots shared with friends later, Cameron returned to his seat. Sofia had fallen asleep while he was gone. She looked so peaceful, he forgot everything else and snuggled up to her from his own seat. He forgot all about Larry as he dozed in his comfortable, padded first class seat. Larry arrived in Copenhagen airport having gotten no sleep and with a back so stiff he could hardly walk.

7

From start to finish, the trip to Castle Elsinore took nearly a full day, involving just about every form of public transportation except for the rickshaw. Customs in Copenhagen Airport took an extraordinary amount of time, stretching tempers microscopically thin. Finally the group piled into a chartered bus for an additional two-hour drive into the countryside.

Exhaustion pretty much overcame the excitement anyone in the group would have been predisposed to feel. So the decidedly different architecture of Copenhagen simply blurred by, not because of the speed of the bus, but due to fatigue. The countryside that separated the city from the village of Kronborg, rolling hills, fertile farmland and dense peat bogs, went almost entirely unnoticed. Only the steep grade of the road approaching the castle roused the travelers, mainly because the bumps disturbed their sleep.

Then the castle came into view.

Everyone who had witnessed it loom into view as they rounded a final bend in the climbing road was awed into wakefulness. Sleepers were soon elbowed and shaken awake as the bus made its final approach. Anger at being disturbed turned to amazement at what lay before them.

Castle Elsinore.

It emerged at the highest point of the Danish coast for miles, more massive a structure than anyone on the bus had ever seen. The four sides of the castle, each many city blocks long, were joined at the corners by tall, white towers. The village lay below in the valley to the west and south. Immediately surrounding the castle were a multitude of lawns, hedges, low walls and topiary. The very eastern edge overlooked a rocky cliff, dropping hundreds of feet to the ocean below. The chill, late fall air, polished by a brisk ocean breeze, afforded the view of a long coastline in the distance: Sweden.

All travel weariness dissolved by the time the bus reached the massive wrought-iron gates guarding the entrance to the ancient estate.

Until that time, no one, not even Cameron, could conceive the reality of his inheritance, of this castle.

Cameron instinctively grabbed Sofia's hand.

"Holy shit!" he muttered.

"The holiest shit there is," Sofia replied softly.

The giant metal gates swung open with a groan, admitting the bus. A pristine, white gravel driveway led to the front door, where the passengers disembarked. They barely had time to choke on the exhaust fumes before an army of formally clad servants emerged from the house and started bustling the luggage away. Each guest was given a three-by-five card upon which was written his or her name and the room in which they would stay. On the reverse side of each card was a small map with directions to each room, which were spread liberally throughout the castle on several floors.

"I am so gonna, like, save this!" Rosenberg shouted to Cameron, waving his card.

Cameron smiled and waved back. As he did, a hand grabbed his shoulder and spun him around.

"Dude. This is so cool." Harry stood there with his girlfriend, Shayne. He gestured at the castle. "I mean, you got a frickin' castle!"

Cameron shrugged. "It's not like I did anything to deserve this."

"Maybe not in this life. But maybe you just hit the karma lottery."

Cameron took in the entire, dizzying scene: a platoon of servants passing luggage into the house like picnic ants; friends and total strangers alike so overwhelmed by their surroundings that they were staggering about as if drunk. This castle was his and he had a few billion (that's with a "b," he constantly reminded himself, not an "m") in the bank. That's a lot of karmic benefit. Like, centuries' worth.

What had his father said about a curse on the men of his family?

Perhaps this was a sign that the curse had lifted. Cameron sure didn't feel cursed.

"Your mother and I are tired." Aunt Claudia's voice momentarily caused Cameron to reconsider the curse issue.

"Yes, dear. This is very exciting, but I need a nap and a bath something awful." Geri gave her son a quick peck on the cheek. "You should get some rest, too."

"Okay, Mom."

"The porter is the man over by the front door." Claudia pointed out a tall, thin man with a rather wide nose who presided over the other help like an orchestra conductor. "His name is Mr. Ginn. So if you need anything while we're asleep, bother him, do not even *think* of disturbing your mother and me."

"Something tells me I'll have better things to do than to worry about you guys." Cameron indicated the castle, implying that it would require exploration. But he was really thinking of Sofia and something he'd been planning for their first moment alone.

"Stop pacing! You're just overtired." Geri was trying to distract Claudia from the anger that had been seething in her since they had arrived. She stalked back and forth in front of an antique anniversary clock, looking like a toy soldier marching to the heavy ticking of the great brass pendulum. Their rooms had been the queen's quarters for hundreds of years, and although the furniture had been updated within the last century, they were still quite luxuriously appointed. At the moment, Geri was swathed in sheets of a criminally high thread count.

"Come to bed and get some rest, Claud."

"Don't call me that!" she snapped. "That's a man's name!"

"I'm sorry."

"I'm sorry," Claudia mimicked back in a whiny voice. "Be sorry about what's gone on here. You and I have been cheated!"

"Come now, Claudia. You're taking this so personally. The will wasn't written to exclude us specifically, it's just some old tradition."

"An old, male-fascist tradition."

"An old, male-fascist not-personally-directed-at-you-so-come-to-bed tradition." Geri sat up in bed, her hands on her hips.

Claudia stopped pacing and crossed to the bed. Sitting, the anger dropped from her face and she reached out to Geri.

"It might as well have been directed at me or you, honey." Geri took her hands. "It's wrong, in any case."

"Then enjoy the control, if that's what you need, for the next couple of days. Buy a car, or a house. I bet Cameron won't mind."

"*Your* son minds everything about me."

"True, but he'll eventually understand. Especially once he's twenty-one and *he* has control of the inheritance." Geri shook her head. "Honestly, how did I get surrounded by so many control freaks. I guess I can get along with you all because I'm not one."

Claudia was looking down at their hands, silent.

"Claud?"

The other woman raised her head slowly. The nickname she usually despised barely registered. Something on the vanity opposite the bed had caught her eye. She stalked over to it.

It was a box of chocolate turtles.

Sofia threw open the glass-paned double doors with the kind of glee usually reserved for movie musicals.

"It's beautiful, Cameron!"

And it was. Breathtakingly so. Beyond the doors lay a small balcony that faced east, over impeccably manicured gardens, unseasonably in bloom with vivid reds and yellows. Gravel paths bordered the green lawns surrounding the estate. On this side, the path ran along the cliff, marked by a set of large boulders. Beyond them was a sheer drop to the ocean below.

Through a window on the opposite corner, the road to the village of Kronborg could be seen. A forest spread out from the western entrance of the estate like a cloak. The road was a seam down the center, leading out of the forest, across a flat patch of dark brown peat bogs and light green farmland, into Kronborg itself.

"Well, call me cynical, but aren't castles supposed to be beautiful? Except for the dungeons, of course."

Theirs had been the king's suite, the most luxuriously furnished in the castle. A fireplace stood against the wall opposite the bed. A great canopy, held up by eight-foot-tall posts, hung above it. All the furniture in the room possessed clawed feet, as did the bathtub, which was trimmed in real gold leaf.

A breeze from the open balcony doors blew a piece of paper from an ornate dressing table onto the floor. Cameron picked it up.

"What's that?"

"Dinner announcement," he replied, reading. "It will be served at eight o'clock in—get this—the 'grand banquet hall.' I like the sound of that!"

"Oooo! I do too!"

Cameron checked his watch. "Let's see, it's nearly four-thirty now." He looked up to the ceiling, calculating. "That means we have plenty of time."

"Plenty of time for what?" Sofia asked with a naughty twinkle in her eye.

"For this," he replied and kissed her, maneuvering her as he did before the window. Releasing her, he took a deep breath. She thought he was preparing for seconds. Instead, he said, "And this." Cameron dropped to one knee.

Out of nowhere, he produced a small velvet box,

about an inch square. Sofia gasped and took a step backward.

"Cameron—"

"Sofia," he interrupted, softly but clearly. "I know things have been upside down and sideways lately. I've been all about the lights but not about the being home."

"Well, that's all over now." Sofia's voice trembled; her eyes were glued to the box Cameron was holding. He smiled.

"Big-time over." He flipped up the lid of the box. Within, a star twinkled, a supernova.

"Marry me," he said through the glare. "I love you. I've loved you since we were kids. In two days, I can have anything I want. But the only thing I need is you. Now.

"Will you marry me?"

He held the box closer to her. She finally looked up into his face. His face was more alive than it had been in months. He had accepted his father's death and moved on.

Into her heart.

"Yes," she said simply. Cameron plucked the ring from the box and slid it onto her extended finger. There were tears in her eyes.

"You know that I love *you*, Cameron," she said, her voice quivering with emotion. "Not your new wealth, not your castle—"

"Good, 'cuz you're signing a prenup anyway."

"Shut up!" She swatted him playfully. He quickly

snapped out of silly mode. "It is you that I love, it is you that I have loved since we were kids and it is you that I need."

"Let's live the rest of our lives together," she told him.

Silently, he led her beneath the great canopy of the bed, where they made love, and it was like a feather falling from a great height onto a landmine.

At that moment, steam began to rise from a section of peat bog below Elsinore. Within minutes, the dark, rich earth began to boil impossibly. Soon after, something as insubstantial as steam but infinitely more dangerous emerged from the earth. Invisible to humans, it nonetheless was made of water and peat, a blue-green and brown thing with tangles of algae for hair.

It was ancient. And like many things resurrected after centuries of sleep, it was angry.

And it wanted revenge.

8

Ophelia, once daughter to Polonius, swept the muck-laden hair from her lifeless eyes. Since she herself was invisible, she could see that which was ordinarily invisible. The world glowed in strange and shimmering colors humans could not perceive. No computer ever showed a more pulsating and vivid landscape. And shining like a beacon, a surreal lighthouse in the distance, was Hamlet.

Her Hamlet.

It was for him that she had once lived. And it was for him that she had died.

And now that she had risen, it was his turn to die for her.

With a thought, her spirit began to glide toward Elsinore, which she recognized with her new, inhuman senses. The only trace of her passage would have appeared to a passerby as a strange dew that suddenly sprang from the ground, and patches of slimy vegetation.

Ophelia was instinctively aware that much time had passed since her death. But this did not concern her. What force was time compared to that of love? Or for that matter, hate? Is hate not the wine fermented from the grapes of love, crushed by those she had trusted? Her father, Polonius; her brother, Laertes, counseled her in contradictions. Hamlet, who had promised his love, gave riddles and reproach instead. And so with cruel words and selfish advice, love had been crushed from her and drained away. Swamp water seemed as good a replacement for lost sweetness as any, and so she drowned.

Existence since then had been a fitful dream. But now she had awakened fully. The wine of her love had turned to hate. It was a draught she intended to share with her beloved Hamlet. Ahead in the castle, the beacon of his soul burned bright. And the color was love.

Steam began to rise from Ophelia's dew-trail. She stopped floating.

To her new senses, Elsinore appeared a star field of love. It was filled with many beings who loved, happily and without much complication.

The ground began to boil once more beneath her.

"As it was for me, so shall it be for others." Ophelia's first words. They were a watery groan, a curse from the jaws of a rotted fish. "Love shall end in death. This I vow."

Ophelia began gliding toward Elsinore once more. She willed herself toward the brightest light among the castle's constellation.

"And you, my dear Hamlet, will finally be mine."

Ophelia's ghost swept through hedges surrounding Elsinore. Rank algae marked her passage. She paused in the hedge maze, for the first time almost nostalgic. Remembering a distant carefree self, she recalled days of leisure on the grounds of the castle. Then Ophelia's finely attuned senses saw the hedges another way. Her special light illuminated the secrets and intrigues that had occurred within the maze: treason, murder and, yes, even discreet liaisons.

Her nostalgia faded. Undeath had given her a new comprehension of her life: she had functioned on a level of a housepet. Praise, the occasional pat on the head, food, the want for attention, the amusement of others—these were pretty much the parameters of life back then. Meanwhile, all around her, secret dramas had been playing out. She could sense them now, in nearly every corner of the hedge maze, vaporous memories only she could perceive.

"What is that smell?"

A young man's voice coming from the hedge before Ophelia surprised her. Her strange new senses had missed someone. She wasn't alone.

"Eeewww!" Now a female voice. "It smells like a sewer!"

Ophelia passed through the hedge to investigate. Algae materialized on the branches as she did so. A slimy strand instantly dropped onto the girl lying below on her back.

"Yuk! What was that?"

She was partially naked. She lay on a garment apparently made of leather and cloth, and on top of her was the young man. He too was partially naked. The ghost was fascinated. She had never seen people in such manner of dress. Or undress, for that matter. Time had indeed passed.

Marc used a finger to wipe the algae from Carla's shoulder.

"Some sort of gunk," he said. He flicked it away like a booger. "Did that smell get stronger?" He sniffed the air and then gagged.

"Take me back inside, Marc," said Carla. She wiggled to roll Marc off of her, but he didn't budge. Of course, he did have her by nearly seventy pounds.

"C'mon baby, just a little while longer. It'll go away."

"But Marc!" Carla whined.

That's when Ophelia realized why she had not initially perceived these two although they had been only feet away: they were not in love! At least not yet. Concentrating on them, she could see a dim glow that would become love if left to flourish.

But it would not flourish.

"C'mon Marc, I'm serious!" Carla was pushing on Marc's shoulders. He just grinned and tried to kiss her.

"What'll you do if I let you go?"

Carla slapped his shoulders lightly. Despite her protestations, the girl was actually enjoying the little game. Ophelia could see the dim glow pulsate slowly.

"I won't charge you with date rape!" But by now, Carla was giggling. She allowed Marc to kiss her on the mouth.

"I could always say *you* raped *me!*"

"Mmmmm . . ." Carla purred. "I'd like to try that."

With that, they were making out again. Their ferocity and passion shocked Ophelia. And angered her. The two were perfectly content, the glow within them becoming brighter.

Ophelia towered above the pair, intending to strike terror in them before killing them.

"If you dare to love, you shall not live!" Ophelia cried.

And nothing happened.

"Are you so used to vengeful ghosts, then?"

Still nothing. Apparently, humans could not hear her. No matter. They would hear each other's screams before they died.

She reached down to destroy the couple, black talons at the end of her rotted fingers. She would pluck the boy's heart from his chest. Then she would delight in the screams of the girl, pinned down by the large boy's dead weight, before ripping her heart out and, for her own amusement, replacing it with the boy's heart.

As Ophelia's fingers plunged into Marc's back, Carla came up for air.

"This is fun, honey, but I think that smell is getting stronger."

And Ophelia's hand passed into Marc's body like the ghost she was. He did not scream in pain. Her fingers did not close around his beating heart.

"Yeah." Marc replied, not noticing Ophelia's hand was buried in his back. "I think something just dripped on me."

She could not touch him. Ophelia pulled her hand out and shook her fist to the sky.

"Why bring me back for revenge if I have no power to claim it?" she screamed. Then she stood by as the couple rose and dressed.

"Ugh," said Carla as she buttoned her blouse. "That was like having sex in the sewer."

"Thanks," Marc replied. He hopped into his jeans, nearly falling over.

"Well, the sex is good, but you know, sex in a sewer kinda sucks."

"C'mon, Carla. I'm starving."

"Of course you are."

Marc turned and walked directly through Ophelia, who stood in their path. The ghost did not move.

What was the point when her effect on the physical world was limited to causing mild physical discomfort? On the other side of Ophelia, Marc stopped and turned around.

"Ew. That was, like, clammy."

"Hey, you have more guck on your jacket." Carla pointed to a strip of algae that had suddenly appeared over his varsity letter. "Here, I'll get that for you."

Carla stepped forward to remove the algae. In doing so, she unwittingly walked into Ophelia, who hoped only that the girl's hair would become entangled in algae.

Instead, Ophelia became entangled in the girl.

One moment, Ophelia was a ghost, seeing the world through her new eyes. The next moment, she was human again, seeing through human eyes.

"Baby? What's wrong?"

Ophelia knew the voice immediately. It was the young man, Marc. Only it sounded different. And very far away. It sounded like a human voice heard by human ears.

"Your lips have turned blue. You okay?" Panic was rising in Marc's voice.

Ophelia turned to see Marc reaching out to her, grasping her shoulders. She felt his large, strong hands. That's when she realized.

She was inside the girl.

Turning her supernatural senses inward, Ophelia perceived the girl's soul as a flickering candle, and saw it was quickly doused by the swamp water of her own presence.

Ophelia could suddenly feel her eyes blink, her lips move, fingers flexing on hands at her side.

"Oh, God, Carla. What's happening?" Marc could only grasp her shoulders in panic, uncertain of what to do.

Ophelia smiled using Carla's face. The blue lips curling up into a grimace caused Marc to step back in disgust.

Then Ophelia opened Carla's mouth to speak. Instead of words, the girl's lungs vomited a great gout of brackish water. Marc suddenly found himself covered in dead leaves and algae, and stinking like a swamp.

He gagged and turned to throw up.

She had a human body, but she still could not speak. But the boy's hold on her shoulders, the smile she had conjured, meant she was a physical being. She was aware of another sensation. It was very familiar, but for the moment she couldn't place it. It would come to her eventually, of that she was sure. For now, perhaps she'd have the boy's heart after all.

While he was still hunched over, Ophelia raised one of Carla's hands and balled it into a fist. She brought it down as hard as she could.

Crack! Marc's spine broke instantly, and he fell to the ground with a grunt. The blow nearly folded him in half backward along the break. He died moments later.

Carla's face smiled, trickling algae from one corner of her mouth.

Not only do I have a body, Ophelia thought. *I have strength.*

She looked down at Marc's crumpled form. The unnatural angle of his back made him look like a discarded marionette.

I haven't ripped out his heart, but this will do.

Ophelia took an unsteady step forward in Carla's body. She maintained her balance.

This girl will be my vessel, she thought. *With her, I shall get my revenge upon Hamlet and all others in Elsinore!*

Stepping over Marc's body, Ophelia set off for the castle. She only made it another five feet. Carla's body fell face forward with a thud. Instinctively, Ophelia clawed at her throat, which suddenly felt quite full. Soon, the body stopped responding altogether.

Water, leaves and mud poured from Carla's mouth. And moments before being forcibly ejected from Carla's body, Ophelia identified the strange sensation she had felt.

Drowning.

9

Dinner began unpromptly at 8:23.

Two impossibly long tables dominated the banquet hall, each place setting of which comprised enough fine china and polished silver cutlery to serve an entire family. Candles lit the entire room as they had in the old days. Bowls and platters laden with all manner of fruits, sauces, relishes, breads, foods both exotic and familiar, were piled high enough to collapse the tables.

The elegance of the surroundings seemed utterly wasted on the American visitors, the staff noted. The informality of the guests' dinner attire affronted their sensibilities, but nonetheless inspired great jealousy and admiration. Young ladies dressed in jeans instead of skirts or dresses, and many of the boys' criminal informality included wearing white T-shirts. Worse still, the chamber reverberated with fart jokes.

Cameron and Sofia joined their families at their designated seats toward the center of the left banquet table. Behind them was a fireplace big enough to fit all of them, standing. His mother sat to his right, with Aunt Claudia beyond her, looking as agitated as Cameron had hoped. A gruff Dr. Paulsen, who scored points with the staff for wearing a tie to dinner (then losing them again when anyone got close to his awful clip), sat on the other side of Sofia. Beside him, sullen, constantly wiggling to stretch his back, sat Larry.

When everyone settled, Cameron stood and addressed the room. He saw several empty places at the table. Unsurprising, he thought. Some people wouldn't adjust to the time change for several days. The missing guests were likely dead asleep in bed right now.

"Friends," he began, "I want to thank everyone for being here tonight. As you all know, it's been a rough year for me and my family."

"Yeah, this is real rough!" Eric shouted out.

Cameron glanced around appreciatively. "Yeah, well, maybe things aren't rough now. But they have been. And as if this trip wasn't evidence enough, I want to thank each and every one of you for your support during this time." He toasted the room. "Thanks."

The assembly broke out into applause, which Cameron soon quieted down.

"This dinner is just the start. Tomorrow we're gonna have a totally badass birthday party, and raise this mother-lovin' medieval roof!"

"Yeah!" Eric said standing and thrusting his glass into the air. Others followed suit and soon applause thundered once more and cheers filled the air. Then began the chanting.

"Woofwoofwoofwoof!" Fists pounded on the table until glasses and plates rattled.

Cameron raised his hands to quiet the crowd. "Wait up! There's more!" He pulled Sofia to her feet and wrapped his arms around her. "Tonight, just before dinner, Sofia and I became engaged."

He grabbed her hand, and she thrust it forward, showing off the ring.

This produced a shocked gasp, then an appreciative round of "Oooo"s at the obvious cost of the ring. A wave of cheers and applause even greater than before swept the room. However, when Sofia turned to her father, she found him as grave as if Cameron had announced her impending death by a slow, painful disease.

"Aren't you happy for me, Daddy?" she asked.

Sofia's father looked at the ring, at his daughter's face, then gave Cameron a particularly dark look. For the moment, the only sound to escape his lips was "Mmmmm . . ."

Cameron was undeterred. He turned to his mother and aunt. His mother looked shocked, but ecstatic. Aunt Claudia, however, shook with outrage. She stood, about to protest, no doubt, but Cameron started speaking before she could start a tirade.

"Hold on, Aunt Claudia, I have more to say." His tone was bright and cheerful.

"Not before—"

He cut her off. "I said I have more to say." This time, his voice wasn't so friendly. Tension suddenly filled the great banquet hall, and everyone wondered if she would create a scene. She saw this in their eyes and started to sit down again.

"No no," Cameron said, his voice honey again. "Please do stand. Mom, you too." He turned to his left. "Dr. P.? Please?"

Sofia's father stood warily. As his mother stood, she was dabbing tears of joy from her eyes. Aunt Claudia stood with her arms crossed tightly across her chest.

Cameron produced three boxes. Sofia looked at Cameron questioningly. He winked. "You'll see," he said.

"These are from me, for my family," he nodded to his mother and Aunt Claudia. "And my family-to-be." He nodded to Sofia's dad. "We don't always see eye-to-eye, but I'm hoping that from now on, we can start too."

He handed the first box to his mother.

"For my mom, the best mother there is."

Geri began to sob. "Oh, honey," she cried as she took the box. In it was a diamond brooch, obviously very expensive. She gasped at its beauty, and held it to her heart to show how much it meant to her.

"I love you, Mom," he said, eliciting a few "awwws"

from the crowd. Cameron then turned to Sofia's dad.

"For you, Dr. P." Then he corrected himself, as if it was just occurring to him. Actually, the flub had been intentional. He handed him the second small box. "I lost a dad this year. I'm hoping by next year, I'll have *you* as my dad."

His eyes still narrow with suspicion, Dr. Paulsen took the box from Cameron. He withdrew the smaller box inside, opened it and pushed the cotton away from the metal object within. He held it up: a tie clip, this one of silver, much more tasteful than the one he currently wore.

"Thought you'd be ready to retire your old one," Cameron joked. Dr. Paulsen examined the new tie clip, as if expecting it to suddenly explode. Almost everyone laughed. No one noticed that Larry wasn't laughing or that his expression was one of panic.

"Last but not least," Cameron said, turning toward his aunt. "And I mean that." Claudia raised an eyebrow at him, showing him she didn't buy it for a second. He didn't care, because of course, he *didn't* mean it. "I know we're not the best of friends, and probably never will be, but you're an important person in my life, and, importantly, in my mom's. And as my father's only surviving relative," he paused ever so briefly to let those words sink in, "I'd like to make this peace offering. Perhaps we can at least be friendly, if not actually friends." He held out the third box.

As he did so, the applause began. First, just a few hands, then, by the time Claudia had opened her box, the applause was thundering and the air filled with more cheers.

When Claudia looked into her box, her ostrich eyes grew wide with horror. She reached into the box and held up a beaded necklace.

Shouting over the crowd, Cameron said to her, "I hope you like it. We all know how much you are into reptiles."

Dangling at the end of the beads was a jade lizard.

Claudia looked at Cameron agape. He just gazed back coolly, the expression of hope that she would like his gift plastered onto his face. She closed her mouth, quickly stuffed the lizard necklace into the box, turned on her heels and marched out of the banquet hall without a word. The applause faltered. Cameron's mom looked confused, rose and followed Claudia out. As Cameron shrugged to Sofia, seeming not to understand what had just happened, Dr. Paulsen placed his new tie clip back into its box and turned to Cameron.

"It is customary to ask the father for his daughter's hand in marriage," he said quietly. Pocketing the box, he turned away slowly and walked toward the exit. Three steps away, he stopped. "Hmmmm . . . Larry!" he called over his shoulder.

Larry's head wagged in surprise. He didn't know his father expected him to follow. Dr. Paulsen grunted once more. Sheepishly, Larry rose and walked to his father. The two left the banquet hall together.

The hall was dead silent now. Everyone looked to Cameron.

"Beats me," he told them. "I guess now you better eat this dinner the staff obviously went to a lot of trouble to prepare. Enjoy."

As they sat to eat, Cameron glanced across the table at Harry. His roommate nodded almost imperceptibly, indicating he had indeed observed Claudia's reaction.

The rest of the dinner was lively, with guests intermittently coming up to congratulate Cameron and Sofia. The awkward moments were soon completely forgotten. When the meal ended, the room was filled with the appreciative sounds of groans, belches and farts commemorating the most sumptuous meal any of the students of Globe University had ever eaten.

For many, it would be their last.

10

As dinner ended, the army of uniformed staff descended upon the tables, clearing them of the meal's remnants like piranha stripping horse carcasses. Soon, the only sign of the banquet was the distant clang of dishes being hand-washed. A cloud of drowsiness descended upon the revelers thanks to copious amounts of food and drink. Most retired to their rooms, barely registering the sun that seemed unwilling to set. It remained low in the sky even at eleven at night.

Cameron and Sofia walked through Elsinore's halls silently, each alone with their thoughts.

"You know, we should really talk to my father," Sofia finally said. "I mean, it's not like the Middle Ages, when daughters were essentially used as currency, but we probably should have broken the news to our families in private instead of ambushing them in public like that."

"I know." Up ahead, Cameron spied Harry and Shayne, admiring some of the architectural features of the hallway. "I suppose I've royally screwed us now. And I'm descended from royalty, so I'm qualified to royally screw things up!"

Sofia laughed. "We'll see. Honestly, I can't imagine why he wouldn't warm up eventually. But we should talk to him sooner rather than later."

She abruptly changed course, heading toward her father's room instead of their own.

"Do you mind doing reconnaissance before I join you?" he asked. "You should probably talk to him on your own, grease the wheels before I show up."

She thought for a moment, then nodded. "Yeah, probably a good idea."

"Okay. I'm gonna catch up with Harry. Meet you back at the room soon."

Kissing Sofia good night, he hurried around the bend toward Harry and Shayne. He found them at a nearby T-junction. Portraits lined the walls to their right and left. To the left, powdered wigs and ruddy complexions indicated time flowing backward. To their right, more modern dress and what appeared to be the subject's actual hair indicated time moving forward.

Electric light fixtures resembling candlesticks were mounted between each portrait. The flame-shaped bulbs even had an element that flickered like candlelight, causing shadows to dance in the narrow gallery.

"Yo, guys!" Cameron said as he caught up with the pair.

"Hey, Cam." The couple had stopped before the portrait of a doughy, pompous-looking individual. It was a full portrait, the man standing in gold-trimmed garb, leaning upon a large cane. His age was hard to tell due to the style. No doubt the man's physical imperfections were minimized, if not eliminated altogether. The practice, Cameron realized, had evolved into airbrushing, and in the most modern sense, digital manipulation of supermodels' photographs for magazine layouts.

Whoever insisted that a simpler, more honest time could be found in the past had not reflected very deeply upon the past, he thought.

"Mind if I join you guys?" he said out loud.

In answer, Shayne slipped her arm in his and the three walked arm in arm, examining the more recent portraits.

"I think these are the past kings and lords of the castle," Shayne said. "Just think, one day you'll be up on this wall, immortalized in this place!"

Cameron realized she was right. Immortality. What a concept! Before last month, he had only hoped to be immortalized in Canton, Ohio, at the Football Hall of Fame. Now, they were discussing his immortalization in a Danish castle. October suddenly seemed centuries in the past.

"So what was the deal with your parents?" Shayne asked. "They didn't seem too thrilled."

"My fault," Cameron admitted. "I broke protocol. They found out the same time you did."

"Bad move," Shayne admitted.

"Yeah," Harry said, trying to sound nonchalant. "I've never seen your aunt so verklempt."

"Maybe she doesn't like lizards as much as I thought."

Shayne was oblivious to the current running between the two friends.

They reached the end of the hallway. The final portrait depicted a thin man who appeared to be in his late thirties. He had a prodigious brow, under which stared dark, blazing eyes. Cameron thought the man looked familiar. He had to tear his eyes away from the man's commanding gaze.

"We'll all deal. Meanwhile, wait till tomorrow's party." They continued on down the passageway. "There's gonna be a DJ, and this band I found over the Internet who'll play until midnight, when I officially turn twenty-one. And that's when the party's *really* gonna start!"

Harry gave him a high five. "Amen to that, brother!"

"We're not just there," Shayne said. "We are *so* there!"

"Awesome. Hey, on another note, can I ask you guys a personal question?" They stopped and separated. Cameron looked around to make sure they were alone. "What's up with Eric?"

Shayne immediately snorted in disgust and turned away. Harry rubbed her arm soothingly.

"It's no big deal, honey," Harry told her.

"You're right," she said. To Cameron's surprise, she said, "A few weeks ago, he asked me out."

Cameron was flabbergasted. "On a date?" His friends nodded. Harry and Shayne had been dating since early high school. Everyone knew that. Then it occurred to him. "Was it a joke? Eric's a chain yanker."

Harry shook his head. "Yeah, ha ha."

"It only happened once," Shayne said. "And I shut him down, but he still gets this look in his eyes sometimes. Gives me the creeps."

"Have you talked to him, Harry?"

"I'm not the 'stay away from my girl,' type as a rule, but yeah, I suggested he was barking up the wrong tree."

"I'm sorry, Cam," Shayne said. "I didn't want to say anything because I know he's your friend and I didn't want to spoil your trip."

"No worries," he told her. "You want me to talk to him? We've known each other since, like, forever." Though they weren't best friends, Eric was his oldest friend on campus, both having grown up in the same Avon suburb.

"Oh no!" Shayne said. "I just think he has a crush and for some strange reason, thought he had a chance."

Cameron just shrugged. Then he was aware of footsteps echoing through the halls, heading in their direction. The three of them nodded in agreement to close the subject of Eric.

Two figures emerged from the center of the T-junction down the hall.

"Hey! Cam!"

"Hey, guys!"

The voices were instantly recognizable, but before anyone could see the faces, two rapid flashes momentarily blinded them. When their vision cleared, Rosenberg and Gyllenhal appeared before them.

"What are you guys doing?" Shayne rubbed her eyes, annoyed.

"We're taking pictures of the place for the school newspaper," Rosenberg said excitedly.

"Yeah, and we've been reading up on the history of the place, too."

"We tracked down your ancestors," Rosenberg continued. "See, there was this prince and his uncle killed his father, the king, and married his mother, the queen."

"Sick stuff," Gyllenhal chirped.

"Somehow, the prince knew, and then the king knew he knew and all hell broke loose."

"What happened?" asked Cameron.

"Something like, 'And then everyone died. The End.'" Rosenberg finished with a shrug.

"Wow. Where'd you find all this out?"

"There's a book set out in the library. Did you know this place had a frickin' library? Hunting rifles on the walls, and stuffed animal heads." Gyllenhal turned to Rosenberg. "I think there's a deer and an elk and a moose."

The red-haired boy nodded, brimming with excitement. "Tons of stuff. Some guy named Shakespeare chronicled the history of the castle."

"I'll have to check that out," Cameron told them. And he meant it. After his inheritance was assured, he planned on spending plenty of time exploring every inch of this place.

"Why is it," Shayne asked suddenly, "that historically, men have often put racks of guns and the results of their violence, severed animal heads, in places like studies and libraries, peaceful and cerebral environments?"

"Yin yang?" Rosenberg chirped.

Gyllenhal hit him on the shoulder. "Shut up. Ever heard of a rhetorical question?"

Shayne snickered at the pair's Laurel and Hardy routine.

"Actually, I'm glad you're here," Cameron told them. "Can you guys do me a favor?"

Rosenberg and Gyllenhal immediately stood at attention, as if asked by a great war general to deliver a crucial message that would save lives.

"Anything, Cam, anything," Rosenberg said.

"I was telling these guys about this great local band I got to play at the party tomorrow night. Anyway, I need to get them money first thing tomorrow, before they'll even come to the castle and set up. Would you take them a check for me?"

The freshmen looked at each other, and nearly hugged each other out of joy. They *had* been dispatched by the general to deliver an important message. They *were* going to save lives!

"You got it!" they said in unison.

"Great," Cameron replied and withdrew a folded, sealed envelope from his back pocket. On it was simply written *The Playaz*. "That's the name of the band. Give this to a guy named Jan, all right?"

"You can count on us, Cam!" Gyllenhal told him and the two trotted off. Before they were out of earshot, they began arguing over who would hold the precious envelope until morning. Soon, their voices faded entirely.

Harry shook his head. "Rosenberg and Gyllenhal are dweebs."

"Nah, honey," Shayne said, still amused by the pair. "I think Rosenberg and Gyllenhal are cute."

Harry yawned at that point.

"Don't know if I'll be able to sleep with all this light, but I'm beat." He turned to Shayne. "Ready for bed, honey?"

She yawned as well. "Yeah, think so."

They said good night to Cameron and continued to their room. Cameron turned back toward the portrait gallery. The eyes of the final portrait stopped him, almost commanding him to stop. He studied it. The feeling of familiarity returned. What was it about this guy? he wondered. He squinted at the painting, as if blurring his vision would make things more clear.

It did.

With his eyes out of focus, the impact of the man's portrait lessened considerably. The intensity returned when Cameron looked at it normally again. Take away the man's eyes, you take away his power, he realized. When he last saw this man, his power had been drained completely. He'd been wizened and blind.

And on his cheek had been a dark, purple stain.

This was his recently dead relative, the previous owner of the castle. The old man who had appeared in his dream.

11

"Are you on crack?!" Claudia shouted. Paul Paulsen winced, but not out of fear; Claudia's breath was very stale and she was right in his face. Her hands worried the beaded lizard necklace like a desperate penitent with a rosary.

"Maybe he's right, Claud," Geri said in a small voice from the edge of the bed where she sat. "I agree that Cameron has made this awkward, that maybe the kids are moving too fast, but maybe this also is a good time to finally show our children some support."

"I said don't call me Claud!" Claudia suddenly ripped apart the necklace and beads scattered onto the floor. Geri shrunk back from her.

"If you were one of my students, Claudia," Dr. Paulsen said quietly, "Mmmm . . . I'd suggest an anger management program."

Like a whip she snapped back at the guidance counselor. "Well, I'm not one of your students, I'm your boss, so watch what you say."

Paulsen shrugged. He was exhausted, by the trip, by the kids' announcement, by the perpetual twilight, beyond the ability to reason or even think deeply. Which is why he had finally broken through and come to his conclusion.

"Mmm . . . I'm not talking to you in a professional capacity, Claudia," he said evenly. "I'm speaking to you as one parent to another. I want my daughter to be happy. Clearly—mmmm . . . and believe me, I would like it otherwise—she is very happy with Cameron. Dating is one thing, but marriage is quite another. I want my daughter in my family, and so, that means I have to be a part of his family. So, I've decided not to fight it anymore."

"Then you're an idiot." Claudia stalked to the opposite side of the room. As she passed the vanity, she picked up her nail file without looking and began to furiously file her nails as she looked out into the distance. She did not intend to speak to Paul Paulsen again.

Realizing he had been dismissed, Paulsen shrugged again. "And you're very sad." He told her. Claudia didn't even twitch. He looked at Geri, who looked up from the bed, pale but encouraging.

"I'm going to go talk to them now. I suggest you do the same before the party tomorrow. Might as well end this mess of a trip on a high note."

He straightened his tie, adjusted his gaudy tie clip and left. Claudia still hadn't turned around.

* * *

Ophelia floated upward toward the blazing beacon that was her Hamlet. But this was a different Ophelia than the one who had risen from the bog. She had retained something from the girl she had possessed. Though visually the world still appeared in her unique spectrum of colors, her mind understood what she was seeing more clearly. For one, she knew the year to be roughly two thousand and three hundred years after she had died. Initially, this filled her full of profound sadness. She wandered the hedge maze for hours, not bothering to float through walls that she could have easily penetrated. For a while, she thought of herself as someone named "Carla," whom she realized was the girl she had possessed. The boy she had killed had been called "Marc." And while her initial instinct that the two were not truly in love was correct, Ophelia (or Carla? Even after the realization she wasn't always completely certain.) still felt sadness at the loss of the couple's burgeoning love.

The sadness that surrounded her almost seemed ready to engulf her, drown her in its essence the way Carla had drowned in hers. The way the living Ophelia herself had drowned amid the dead leaves and grass and mud. She knew she had to lift herself above the sadness. She had to focus on revenge. And Hamlet. With a burst of determination she thought: *Melancholy kinda sucks.*

The words soothed Ophelia. She began to float faster. Then she stopped. "Melancholy *kinda sucks?*" What kind of language was this? It was so . . . inelegant. Very unbefitting a woman once destined to be princess. It was so . . . common. Distasteful it seemed at first; however, the thought and feeling had eradicated her sadness. A boldness coursed through her. She had shaken free of her possession-induced melancholy.

She repeated the words one more time.

"Melancholy sucks!" Then, "And it doesn't just *kinda* suck, it *totally* sucks!"

Ophelia spoke aloud with the utmost conviction, but the only audible result was a watery wheezing in the air. Still, she was emboldened, a thrill running through her insubstantial body. She was ready to return to the matter at hand: her vengeance.

With that in mind, another aspect of her mission became clear: she could not use just any vessel to rend Hamlet's soul from his physical body. As she was Hamlet's love, the instrument of her vengeance needed to be his current life's love. Only in the poetry and symmetry of the act of using his lover to kill him would give Hamlet's soul over to Ophelia, for her eternal companionship.

And so would her vengeance, against Hamlet, against love, be fulfilled.

These thoughts lifted Ophelia skyward once more, toward the tower room shared by the doomed lovers. Ophelia gave a passing thought to her living rival.

The bitch is going down. With her focus on the tower, she didn't notice the contemporariness of the thought.

"He wasn't there," Sofia told Cameron when he returned to the room.

"What did Larry say?" he asked.

"Nothing. He just heard Dad's door close and him walking away."

"Probably went to talk to my mom and Aunt Claudia," Cameron said, hugging her as they both stood on the balcony. It was nearly midnight and the sun still hovered at the horizon. "They're probably planning on how to separate us forever."

"God, I hope not." Then, a moment later, Sofia said, "Hey what's that smell?"

The stench of rot suddenly filled the balcony.

"Uck," Cameron gagged. "Smells like Godzilla farts."

They giggled as he pulled Sofia away from the window. He figured that they had gotten a rank gust of wind from the ocean.

Suddenly, Sofia turned cold in his arms. And clammy. She twisted suddenly, as if standing on a turntable. Her eyes had gone completely black. So had her lips. Algae, leaves and maggots twisted and writhed in her hair. Foul water gushed from her lips.

"Sofia?" Despite his fear, he did not back away from her. "Oh, God!"

In the pause between utter confusion and action, Sofia's cold hands came up to clutch Cameron's throat. He couldn't breathe.

"Sof—" he tried to croak out, but his windpipe was completely blocked. Soon, the damage would be permanent, as would his resulting death.

It had taken the entire walk, but Dr. Paul Paulsen had finally come to terms with what he would say to Sofia and Cameron. At the time, his speech to Claudia and Geri, about giving the kids a chance, had been sincere. But on the way over, he realized it had not been. Not entirely. Claudia's behavior had, ironically, tipped the scales in their favor. She was so ugly, inside and out, and irrationally against the children's happiness that he realized he could not allow himself to be the same.

Still, it took some effort to get excited about welcoming Cameron unconditionally into his family. Was he doing this because he meant it? Or was he simply reacting to Claudia's bile?

In the end, it didn't matter. The gesture was necessary, at least to get through the next few days in a civil manner. And perhaps, things would work out anyway. After all, Cameron wasn't such a bad kid. Dr. Paulsen simply wanted better for his daughter. But what was "better" now, considering Cameron's inheritance? Certainly she wouldn't want for anything in her life as long as she was with Cameron. And if there was a problem between them, no doubt she'd meet it head-on. Sofia was no shrinking violet. Not like Geri, Cameron's mom.

So that was in Cameron's favor. He evidently wasn't going all Freudian with the need to marry someone like dear old Mom. Perhaps there was hope after all.

This helped him with another realization he had come to recently. Larry was growing into a strange and bitter young man. And it had been very much his fault. Letting go of Sofia would give him time to focus a bit more on Larry, keep him from becoming any more emotionally stunted than he was. Yes, after this, Larry would start enjoying a bigger piece of the fatherly love pie.

Dr. Paul Paulsen smiled to himself. *I better watch it,* he thought. *Or they'll revoke my curmudgeon membership.*

With that thought, Paulsen found himself at the door to Cameron and Sofia's room. He stood for a moment, cleared his throat, adjusted his tie and clip, then raised his hand to knock on the door. Before he could, a loud crash sounded from inside the room.

Curious, he thought, and knocked anyway.

There was no reply but yet another crash and the sounds of a scuffle.

"Mmmmm . . . you guys okay in there? It's Sofia's dad."

The only response was a choked cry.

Without another thought, Paulsen opened the door and flew into the room. His worst nightmare greeted him.

Cameron and Sofia were rolling around on the ground, their hands at each other's throats. He was killing her: her lips were already black, her tongue swollen and protruding from her mouth.

"Get off of her!" he yelled.

Hurrying over to them, he grabbed Cameron's hands, easily removing them from his daughter's throat. Cameron tried to choke something out, but couldn't speak. Sofia remained determined to crush the life out of Cameron.

"It's okay, honey. Daddy's here." He tried to pull his daughter away, but her grip was even stronger than Cameron's. He snarled at the boy. "I should let her kill you, you son of a bitch, Mmmmmm—"

His characteristic grunt suddenly choked to an end. One of Sofia's hands released Cameron and clutched at her father. He stood to pull away, dragging Sofia with him. Now, all three of them were struggling together. Paul Paulsen's eyes were wide with terror and pain.

Cameron locked his hands together and brought them up sharply beneath Sofia's elbow. She released his throat and collapsed to the ground, gasping for breath. Impassively, Sofia turned all her attention to Paulsen, and began to strangle her father with both hands. He could only struggle ineffectually against her.

As she stepped forward to gain more solid footing, Sofia tripped on Cameron's legs. She fell toward her father, pushing him backward toward the balcony window. With a gurgling cry, Sofia pushed and her father literally flew out of the window.

From where Cameron lay on the floor, he could almost see Dr. Paulsen hang for an infinite moment before he plummeted downward. He fell silently; Sofia had crushed his larynx. The crackle of breaking branches rose from below the tower.

Sofia turned back toward Cameron, who scrambled backward on his feet to escape. She reached out. Then fell forward, her eyes rolled up into her head, muddy water gushing from her mouth.

12

Cameron didn't know what to do. Dr. Paulsen had just fallen a hundred feet from the tower. And at Cameron's feet, Sofia lay inexplicably drowning after having tried to kill him. Black water seeped from her mouth on either side of her swollen tongue, around which she struggled to breathe, choking instead.

"NO!!!" Cameron shouted and dropped to his knees. He couldn't understand quite what had happened but he wasn't going to let Sofia die. Not like this. Not with him watching like an idiot.

First, he flattened her tongue as best he could. Already, the swelling was receding. That's when he noticed the overall change. Her eyes were hazel edged in red, not black. The maggots in her hair had all died and the leaves and algae that had swirled like living things lay limp. And the smell. The sewage smell had faded almost to nothing.

He paused another second to consider what it meant. And then another when he realized her father likely lay dead at the base of the tower below. A hand reached up and clutched his collar. He jerked back instinctively and shouted in surprise.

Sofia was looking at him, her hand meant to attract his attention, not to kill him.

"I'm gonna save you, baby," he said to her and pinched her nostrils closed with one hand. The taste of the brackish water he sucked out of her lungs nearly made him vomit. But he held on. Sofia struggled with him to remain conscious.

"Breathe, baby, breathe," he said between intervals of drawing water from her lungs.

Finally, she coughed, reflexively sitting up as her muscles contracted, forcing the last of the water from her lungs.

"That's right, Sofia, get it all out." Cameron stroked her hair, still slimy from the muck tangled in it. But now, he did not notice. Her tongue had returned to normal size and no longer blocked her throat. It and her lips had faded from black to a light purple, indicating her blood was receiving oxygen again.

"I'm going to put you on the bed, okay?" he asked softly. She nodded through a coughing spasm so he gently lifted her and placed her on the soft bed. A murky stain immediately began to spread around her body from the moisture that soaked her clothes.

"You'll be okay, Sof. Sssshhhhh . . ." Her coughing was finally quieting down. He did feel like she would be all right. But would she really? Would *they*? Her father was dead. She had, for all intents and purposes, killed him. Oddly, Dr. Paulsen had saved Cameron's life; if he hadn't appeared when he did, Sofia would have killed him. He rubbed his own throat, still sore from Sofia's attack.

Sofia rolled over on her side, and was soon breathing steadily. He watched her for several minutes. She coughed a few times, but remained asleep.

Hoping she would be all right without him, Cameron fled the room.

I killed my father, she thought.

Ophelia wandered the halls of Castle Elsinore. Though its layout was familiar to her, she was lost. In the halls. Inside her mind. More specifically, she was lost inside the scraps she had retained of Sofia's mind.

Not my father, Ophelia corrected herself. *Her* father.

Despite the assertion, Ophelia struggled to differentiate herself from Sofia. The girl had been strong. Too strong. Despite Ophelia's ability to control the girl's body, and how close she came to freeing Hamlet's soul from Cameron (*my fiancé? I am to be married to Cameron?*), the girl had forced Ophelia from her body before she was dead. Sofia was alive now;

she could feel it. And like before, Ophelia was struck by a profound sadness, for the loss Sofia would feel if she succeeded in slaying Cameron and for the death of Sofia's father. Ophelia wanted to believe the old fool's intercession had tipped the scales, allowing Sofia to overcome her. But Ophelia knew the truth: Sofia was just too strong. Ophelia would have to become much stronger before she would be able to overcome Sofia's will and claim Hamlet's soul as her own.

And strength she would draw. Looking about her with her preternatural sight, she could sense all the other souls in the castle, all the bright lights just waiting to be snuffed in fulfillment of Ophelia's curse. Love will not survive.

Uh uh. No way. WAY no way!

Ophelia smiled to herself at the new shape of her thoughts. There was the power—the power of defiance, the power of freedom, the power of independence. This was the power she drew from her victims. In death, this made her feel more alive than she had while living. She thought back to her father, long dead and resting peacefully, but no doubt boringly, in sanctified ground. What would he say if he saw his daughter Ophelia now? Would he treat her like the simple child she had, to be fair, actually been?

No, things would be different, and Hamlet would bear witness to her transformation. When they were together again, there would be no more of this "get thee to a nunnery" crap. He was going to find out who wore the leggings in the family.

Okay, so modernity hadn't seeped all the way into Ophelia, but she was content to know that, wording aside, she had expressed a thoroughly modern thought.

And there was more where that came from, more power, to be provided by the hapless souls around her.

"I think a toilet overflowed somewhere," came a squeaky voice from around the next corner, heading in her direction. Ophelia had gained enough knowledge of present times to finally start taking offense at people's comments about one of the telltale signs of her manifestation.

Two gawky youths appeared before her. Both were male, and impervious to her powers, but at least she could cause them discomfort. She waited in the hallway until the red-haired boy walked through her, but then glided along with them, keeping to the boy at all times.

"Dude," Rosenberg said suddenly. "Did you hock a loogey on my neck?"

"Of course not!" answered Gyllenhal. "Hey, wait." They stopped, with Ophelia still invisibly shrouding Rosenberg. Gyllenhal reached up and grabbed a dead leaf from the nape of his friend's neck.

Rosenberg giggled and pulled away. "Dude! Stop that!"

Gyllenhal ignored him and held up the leaf. "Here's your loogey." He searched the ceiling behind them. "I guess this place has got leaks. Hey, here's another." This time he plucked the leaf from Rosenberg's arm. At his touch, Rosenberg nearly shrieked and collapsed against the wall, giggling hysterically.

"What's with you?"

"I don't know," Rosenberg answered as he pulled himself together. "I'm just super ticklish all of a sudden."

"Oh, really?" An evil glint shined in Gyllenhal's eyes. He held up his index finger as if it were a weapon. "So, would it tickle you if I did . . . this?" and he quickly poked Rosenberg in the side.

"Ow!" he cried, but held his side in a spasm of laughter. "Stop it, Pete!"

But the protestation fell on deaf ears. "What about . . . this?" He jabbed his finger into his stomach. Rosenberg nearly lost his balance trying to block Gyllenhal. He was losing his breath laughing.

"This is like a superpower!" Gyllenhal struck a heroic stance with his index finger held up and announced imperiously: "I am Tickle Man!"

"Take that! And that! And that!" With each "that," he poked Rosenberg, sending him into greater and greater anguished hysterics. The whole time, Rosenberg panted for him to stop. Finally, Rosenberg tried to pull away, but Gyllenhal followed him.

"You will not escape me, villain!" As if he were a great swordsman, he chased Rosenberg down the hall, jabbing under his armpit, on the side of his neck and everywhere. Tears streamed down Rosenberg's face, he was laughing so hard.

Ophelia did not follow them. Though she was unable to possess the boy, her presence had obviously had some effect on him in the form of his heightened sensitivity. And she had gained a small amount of knowledge from him—his name and that of his immature companion. And, like many others, had made a determination about them.

Rosenberg and Gyllenhal were children.

Casting her perceptions like a trawling net across the castle, she spied several nearby lesser beacons. Each meant a couple in love. And each meant a fresh victim for Ophelia's wrath.

13

A bleary-eyed Harry opened the door to his and Shayne's room about fifteen minutes later. Cameron was frantic, not the least reason for which was because he had gotten lost several times on his way there. So many hallways and staircases to negotiate. And every moment that passed meant an opportunity for someone to discover Dr. Paulsen's body.

"What's up, bro?" Harry yawned. He could tell his friend was agitated but was still too drowsy to react properly.

"Get on your clothes and come with me," Cameron whispered.

"Oh man, I just got to sleep."

"This is really important."

Harry seemed about to protest again, then he woke up enough to see the urgency in Cameron's eyes. They were even more intense than the night he had concocted the bizarre murder scenario.

"Hold up," he said, and closed the door. Cameron paced frantically in front of the door for what seemed like an hour. When the door opened, only a minute had gone by.

"What?" Harry said, but Cameron didn't answer.

"Just come on," he said, motioning for Harry to follow him. Harry didn't even bother asking again what was going on.

They soon found themselves outside. After a few crunching steps on the white gravel that trimmed the paths, Cameron veered onto the lawn beside it. Their footsteps immediately fell silent.

Sticking close to the side of the castle, they headed north along the path. Windows and various entrances appeared every so often. At first, Cameron would stop, signal for Harry to remain silent, and he would peer into a window. Each one was dark. Soon, he appeared certain no one would be looking out of any of the first-floor windows, or spilling out of a doorway into their path, and Cameron picked up the pace.

The air was cold and Harry shivered. Cameron had not told him to bring a jacket. The dim light and the silence, save for the distant crashing of waves on the coast below the cliffs, gave the night an air of wrongness, like the nervous stillness of a solar eclipse.

Finally, they neared the base of the tower. Cameron instinctively looked up, to make sure that Sofia had not awakened. The balcony doors were closed, their windows dark.

"Oh geez," Harry said, bringing Cameron's attention back to the ground. He followed his friend's gaze. A shiny black shoe jutted from behind a clump of bushes at the base of the tower. A thin strip of pale flesh, between the top of a black sock and the cuff of black suit pants, seemed to possess a fluorescent glow.

"Dr. Paulsen?" Harry asked, both incredulous and horrified, as they neared the body. One of the bushes was nearly flattened, displaying numerous broken branches. The body had obviously landed on it, then rolled to the ground behind. Dr. Paulsen lay facedown, his limbs splayed at wild angles.

"What the hell happened?" Harry demanded.

Cameron explained Sofia's bizarre fit, even showing him the bruises that had blossomed on his own neck. He related how Dr. Paulsen had burst into their room, wrestled them apart and then became Sofia's victim in his stead.

"It was crazy, Har," Cameron said, rubbing his throat. "It wasn't Sofia at all. She looked like some zombie. Then, just like that, she was back again. It was crazy," he repeated.

Now it was Harry's turn to pace frantically back and forth.

"What are we gonna do, Cam? Oh my God!" He stopped to gape at the corpse again, then turned away abruptly and started to gag.

Cameron grasped his friend's shoulder.

"I didn't ask you here to freak you out, or have you lose it on me, Harry." His friend straightened and attempted to compose himself. "We're gonna hide the body."

Harry studied his face for a moment, then the look of horror returned.

"No, no, uh uh," he said. "Okay, driving your aunt crazy to make her admit that she murdered your father, that's one thing. That's revealing a murder. But covering *up* a murder? No way."

Cameron stopped his friend again, this time holding him firmly by both shoulders.

"It was an accident," he staid emphatically. "An accident I *never* want Sofia to know about. I'm having a hard enough time with my own father's death, imagine how I'd feel if it were my fault!"

Harry tried to pull away, but Cameron wouldn't let him go.

"I will do *anything* to protect Sofia from that. *Anything.*" Harry finally stopped struggling. Cameron's icy blue eyes froze him in place. "I don't know how this is ultimately going to play out, but we have to hide him until I can figure something out. Maybe this is my wild card to deal with my aunt, I don't know. But I would rather Sofia thought I killed her father than that she did it. Understand?"

Numbly, as if he were waking up all over again to a knock at his door, Harry nodded.

"Where, then?" he asked.

Cameron scanned the area. In the distance, he saw a small shed. He pointed to it.

"There," he said. "Stand by, I'm gonna go check it out."

Harry nodded, still clearly on the verge of panic. But he didn't bolt as Cameron trotted away.

As Cameron approached the shed, his eyes darted left and right to make certain he wasn't being observed by anyone except Harry.

The shed was a low wood building, about ten feet long and eight feet wide. A sliding door was its only entrance. A padlock secured the place. Walking around it, Cameron peered into a window set in the center on one of the longer sides. In the dim light shining through a window on the opposite wall, Cameron could see vague white rectangular shapes piled on the floor. He guessed they contained topsoil or mulch. The implements hanging neatly against one wall—various small claws and trowels, a large set of shears and, leaning next to them, a tall spade—confirmed that this was the gardening shed.

It would do for now. He trotted back to Harry and told him the plan.

Harry almost finally lost it when Cameron told him to grab Dr. Paulsen's legs. He didn't want to touch the body. Neither did Cameron, but there was hardly a choice.

Finally, Harry calmed down long enough to do his part. Gagging again, he lifted the corpse's legs. At the same time, Cameron hooked his hands under the dead man's armpits and lifted.

Dr. Paulsen was not a big man, but apparently he was quite dense.

Over the next fifteen minutes, Cameron and Harry struggled to carry Dr. Paulsen over to the shed. They finally set him down in front of the sliding door.

"It's locked," Harry said, panic again turning his voice up an octave.

"No worries," Cameron replied and lifted a large rock that lay beside the path. He struck the padlock several times, once producing sparks. On the third try, the latch broke and the padlock tumbled to the ground.

Grabbing the handle, Cameron slid the shed door open. Its screech pierced the night like a Rodan-sized seagull. Harry bolted at the sound, but Cameron ran after him and tackled him.

"It's okay, Harry," he told him. "We're almost there. No one heard." He didn't know that for sure, but he apparently convinced Harry, who nodded. They both rose and returned to the shed, where Harry, having apparently been pushed past some sort of mental limit, calmly made two potentially distressing observations.

Peering inside the shed, he saw that besides a few bags of mulch, hoses, a wheelbarrow and various gardening tools, the shed was nearly empty.

"There's nowhere to hide the body," he pointed out. Then he lifted the broken door latch from the ground. "And even if there was, we couldn't lock the door again. He'll never last here."

Cameron examined the door itself. Sure enough, he had torn the entire assembly out of the wood. Not only was the damage irreparable, but it would no doubt attract attention.

He snatched the latch assembly from Harry and threw it to the ground in frustration. As he struggled to calm himself, the roar of blood in his ears subsided, giving way to the pounding of the surf below the nearby cliffs.

He knew what to do, at that moment. But it was a crucial moment, because in a way, he would be crossing a line. And he didn't know if he'd be able to cross back. Then he remembered his own words.

He said he'd do anything to protect Sofia from the knowledge that she had killed her father.

And if that meant that she never saw her father again, then so be it.

"Come on Harry, let's load up the wheelbarrow. It'll be easier."

Harry instantly saw what Cameron had planned and blanched. But he too realized that under the circumstances, they only had time to consider this one, simple and absolute choice.

When Cameron returned to his room later, he found Sofia sleeping peacefully. For the rest of the night, which only got dark for an hour around three A.M., he watched her chest rise and fall regularly. Her body still faintly reeked of decaying vegetation, but ultimately it either dissipated or he got used to it and couldn't smell it anymore. The whole time, he didn't even doze once. Finally, he got up and showered and dressed before she awoke. He pulled on a mock turtleneck to cover the fading bruises on his neck. Luckily, the air was brisk so his outfit would not look out of place.

In bed, Sofia groaned and rolled over. He immediately went to her side. His fingers instinctively went to stroke her hair, which was matted and tangled from last night's episode.

"What happened?" she asked groggily.

"I'm not sure, honey," he said softly. One of the thoughts that kept him awake was that she might remember last night's events. If so, then his efforts to protect her would have failed, and his actions would probably serve only to make things worse.

But for once, luck was on his side.

"I . . . don't . . . know. . . ." she said slowly, failing to pierce the veil that had dropped over her memories of the last twelve hours. "We were enjoying the view . . . and then nothing." She sniffed the air, and put a hand up to touch her scalp. "What's this crap all over me?" she asked.

"Um, I tried to revive you by putting you in the shower, to run cold water on you," he told her, barely knowing what words would emerge from his mouth until they did. "But something was wrong with the plumbing, all this scum came out of it."

"Gross!"

"Yeah, well, you never can tell with these old places. Anyway, it must have worked, 'cuz you seemed okay, even if you didn't wake up. You didn't seem . . . sick anymore." He picked a leaf out of her hair. "You slept okay. I watched you all night."

"I remember bits of dreams," she said suddenly. Cameron tensed. Did her father feature in any of her dreams? He hoped not. "They were weird dreams. I remember some girl named Ophelia. And there was some guy, named Hamlet. They were in love. But something went . . . wrong." She was searching her cloudy mind again. But that was all that came.

"Don't worry about it," Cameron told her. "There was probably something in the food last night. I'll talk to Mr. Ginn at breakfast."

"Yeah, would you?" she asked. Then she rose. "The plumbing's working now?"

"Yup, tested it myself," he said brightly. "Smell me," he said, "I'm clean."

She smiled, definitely with lower wattage than usual, but it was a Sofia smile nonetheless, and went to take a shower.

He waited, almost beginning to relax as a gentle ocean breeze blew in from the balcony. Then he heard the waves crashing, sounding more angry than ever. Rising, he shut the balcony doors. It muffled the ocean's roar, but didn't block it out completely. Cameron no longer found the sound exciting or romantic or powerful.

Now, it just sounded like an accusation.

This sea change had occurred last night, as he and Harry dumped the body of his fiancé's father out of a wheelbarrow and over a cliff. The roar of the surf drowned out any sound the body may have made hitting the water. The ocean took the body then. And its crashing waves now served only to remind Cameron of the secret it held.

14

As Cameron and Sofia shambled through the halls to breakfast, they ran into many of their friends. Low-key greetings were exchanged. There are few "morning people" in a place where night never seems to end. Despite the early hour, a maid was already pushing a housekeeping cart from room to room.

Not a few male eyes turned toward the housekeeper. She was pretty, dark blond and buxom. Not at all like the old, misshapen crones who intruded on a late-morning sleep at the Motel 6.

In the dining room, many guests were already scooping forkfuls of pancakes, eggs of all sorts, bacon (in both its hamlike European style and the more "American" streaky bacon), stewed tomatoes, mushrooms and more into their mouths. A steam table contained all that and more: porridge, fresh fruits, muesli and other cereals, and a variety of juices and smoked kippers in addition to the more common cooked meats. The fish were a little too strange for the American palate and remained untouched by all but the most adventurous.

To Cameron's relief, Dr. Paulsen's absence drew scant notice. Sofia seemed unconcerned. Larry had not yet come to breakfast. No doubt he was waiting on his father. In fact, less than half the group were present. Cameron noticed that Bernie and Maddy had not yet arrived, nor had Marc and Carla. It occurred to him that Marc and Carla had missed last night's dinner as well, but the appearance of his mother and Aunt Claudia caused him to drop the thread immediately. He wasn't in the mood for them, so he asked Sofia if they could avoid his family for the moment and join Harry and Shayne, who he spied entering the room. Harry looked terrible. Apparently he hadn't slept last night either.

Cameron wondered how he felt about the ocean's roar right about now.

"I think I got it now!"

Bernie had finally found the right position for the too-small shower curtain. If he was right, most of the water would stay in the tub, and not flood the bathroom floor. But he wasn't absolutely certain. With the showerhead on a bendy hose instead of mounted above his head, a tub that would seem too narrow for a career bulimic and a postage stamp of a shower curtain, Bernie was very close to spending the rest of the trip, let alone the rest of the day, au naturel.

"Jesus, will you hurry up! Breakfast will be over!" Maddy had been up for an hour and a half, and ready to go within thirty minutes of rising. While Bernie played with the shower as if it were a Rubik's Cube, she hummed Backstreet Boys tunes and devoured three chapters of a novel.

Someone knocked at the door.

At the same time, a blast of water from the showerhead knocked the curtain out of the way, ensuring the bathroom would be fit only for Noah's Ark if Bernie continued.

"Screw it!"

Jumping from the shower, Bernie threw on some boxers. A loud thump came from the bedroom.

"Hey Maddy, what—?" But Maddy wasn't there. Instead, a housekeeping cart lay on its side just inside the closed chamber door. Towels had spilled in a pile beside it and a housekeeper knelt with her back to Bernie, trying to pick things up. Or so it seemed.

Bernie had seen this maid before. She was as hot from the back as she was from the front. And he wanted to see her front. He quickly glanced around the room. Apparently, Maddy had left for breakfast without him.

"Hey, let me help you," Bernie said, walking toward her. He thanked his good fortune that Maddy was gone and that he was only wearing his boxers. His solid but well-sculpted physique was shown off to maximum effect. And in the long run, having fewer clothes to remove would save some time. He might even make breakfast. With appetite to spare. Maybe the housekeeper would show him the proper way to use the shower. *Porno movies contained scenes like this*, he thought.

The housekeeper, whose name had been Frieda, stood and turned. And the porno movie ended abruptly. As the housekeeper's big chest swiveled his way and rose, something in the pile of towels below commanded Bernie's attention. An eye staring out between a bath mat and rumpled hand towel. A lifeless eye. Maddy's eye.

"What the—?"

That's when he saw the housekeeper. More arresting than the bulge in her uniformed chest was the swollen, black tongue protruding from her mouth. Black eyes—staring and lifeless in their way as Maddy's—but animate and aware. Of him.

Frieda, who in her dying gasps would think of herself as Ophelia, reached toward Bernie. He ducked her easily, with the trained instincts of an NFL-bound football player. He dropped past her to his knees, elbowing her in the stomach as he did so. It was like elbowing a brick wall, but the housekeeper went down. *Fuck the penalty*, he thought fiercely. His large hands began to tear at the towels to uncover Maddy.

He couldn't tell if she was breathing or not. Her chest was underneath the cart itself. Slipping a hand between the floor and the edge of the cart, he tried to lift it from her. He would need better footing.

This sucker must weigh a ton, he thought.

"Hang on Maddy. Please!" he cried out loud and braced himself to heave the housekeeping cart away from his girlfriend.

Out of the corner of his eye he saw the housekeeper rise and come toward him. He ignored her. The wide receiver had a least a hundred pounds on the girl, and if she tried to scratch his eyes, well, he'd tear off her hands.

She didn't go for his eyes.

Bernie felt a sharp blow between his shoulder blades and the crackle of breaking bones. All sorts of sensations hit him at once: excruciating pain, a sudden feeling of fullness in his chest, and an eerie stillness. The blood that had throbbed angrily in his temple moments before ceased entirely. He leaned back and looked down at an object that was pulsating before him.

The housekeeper's hand, which she had thrust through his back and out of his chest, held his still-beating heart. With lungs full of blood, Bernie could only gurgle at the sight of it twitching its last.

Darkness took Bernie then, the smell of sauerkraut filling his nostrils. He fell forward onto a pile of towels. The suddenly lifeless body of Frieda fell with him.

* * *

"This *totally ROCKS!*"

Profound sorrow and exultation swirled within Ophelia. She rose from Frieda's body, arms stretched, spiraling upward through floor after floor of Castle Elsinore. Her body gave off a shower of sparks only her own eyes could see. However, on the floor and ceiling of each level she passed through, a patch of boiling water suddenly appeared. One member of the staff, having a secret smoke in one of the unoccupied floors, saw a blur shoot upward through the ceiling. *Or was it the smoke?* he wondered. He looked at the joint glowing at his fingertips and had a second thought. *Cool*.

Ophelia/Carla/Frieda/Maddy didn't notice him or anything else outside of her own radiance. Having possessed the housekeeper in the hallway, she had surprised Maddy by ramming the girl with the cart, crushing her with it. Unfortunately, in her excitement, she had nearly killed the girl, whom she had planned on possessing as well. Ophelia was no longer trapped in a body until it expired; she could leap from body to body if she wished. However, Maddy was fading fast and Ophelia was preparing to absorb as much power and emotion as she could when Bernie interrupted her.

He was a strong one, to be sure. And with her increasing awareness of modern custom and fashion, she had the time to think how hot he looked in his boxers. Strong, too, judging by the blow he delivered without looking; the time wasted admiring what would soon be lifeless flesh had given him a chance to act.

Even as he hopelessly tried to wake his girlfriend, who was by now beyond his help, Ophelia had paused. Broad back. Strong arms. She had wondered if the flesh she currently inhabited would survive long enough to sample the physical pleasures the youth in front of her was surely capable of.

But that was Frieda's voice in her head, not her own. Ophelia resisted. She would have Hamlet, and no one else. Maddy had concurred. Apparently, she'd given Bernie a whirl and had been unimpressed. Besides, the black swarms were returning, signaling the imminent death of the housekeeper's physical self.

And so, she had shown Bernie the shape of his heart.

Later that morning, Rosenberg and Gyllenhal arrived at the nearby town of Kronborg, having walked from the castle. At the center of town, they stood on the corner of a quaint shopping district, in the middle of a town that seemed barely changed from medieval times. Except for the nearby Starbucks.

They had no idea where to go next. Worse, none of the signs were in English.

"Oh great, now what?" Rosenberg and Gyllenhal each turned in place, looking for something, anything, that would lead them to the flat where they could find The Playaz. It was supposedly right around the corner from where they now stood, down a nearby alley.

But Rosenberg couldn't read the directions he had written down.

"You bunghole," Gyllenhal said. Even he couldn't decipher his friend's handwriting.

"Don't call me a bunghole," Rosenberg whined back.

"Okay . . . bunghole."

Rosenberg shot him a dirty look. Gyllenhal responded by raising his index finger into the air.

"Don't make me summon Tickle Man!" he said, an evil smile on his lips.

Rosenberg immediately clenched his arms to his sides, blocking access to his armpits.

"Don't even think about it!" he warned.

Gyllenhal didn't attack, but he didn't put his finger down, either. Rosenberg continued to stand, muscles taut to reduce ticklishness. A classic Mexican standoff. Of sorts.

Soon, they tired and realized there was only one thing to do next.

"Latte?" Gyllenhal asked.

The pair crossed the street and walked into the Starbucks. Ordering their drinks was easy—venti meant the same thing world over, apparently. Paying for the drinks was another, awkward problem, that entailed Gyllenhal fanning all his money onto the counter and having the cashier point at the denominations that were necessary.

"Aren't we supposed to be using Euros?" Rosenberg asked as they took stools by the front window.

Gyllenhal shrugged. "That you even know they exist scares me."

They sipped their lattes quietly for a few minutes, contemplating how they were going to accomplish their mission. If they failed, Cameron would want to kill them. He had shown them so much faith and respect by even asking them in the first place. If Cameron was Batman, they both felt like Robin—an issue that they had even discussed to avoid arguments later. Gyllenhal was the original Robin, the one who became Nightwing in *The Teen Titans*, and Rosenberg was the second one, the one that was later kidnapped and murdered by the Joker.

"Hey, cool!" Gyllenhal said suddenly. In a lower voice, he directed Rosenberg's attention to a newspaper beside him. It showed two men, each holding a shovel, standing on either side of what appeared to be a corpse. An inset showed a closeup of the corpse's face. She was chocolate brown, and looked to be sleeping rather than dead.

"Very cool!" Rosenberg replied, tilting his head at an uncomfortable angle to view it properly. The text was all in Danish, so they couldn't read the caption.

They barely noticed the hand holding the newspaper: slim, well-manicured, rose-red nail polish. But the woman reading the paper noticed the boys.

"Hey, aren't you guys up at the castle?" She spoke with a local accent, but not too thick to understand.

Rosenberg and Gyllenhal straightened up with some embarrassment for being caught reading over someone's shoulder.

"Yeah, hi, sorry," Gyllenhal said. She looked familiar, but neither could place the face.

"No worries," the woman said casually. She smiled easily. "I am up there, too. I am Kay. I am here with Eric. You know Eric?"

The boys introduced themselves.

"Hey, you're the eBay chick, right?"

Gyllenhal swiftly poked him in the side, causing Rosenberg to fall off his stool, clutching himself, giggling.

"No manners," he said. "Yeah, we know Eric. He's on the football team. We are too, you know."

Rosenberg set himself back onto his stool, sniffing back some laughter. He pushed Gyllenhal lightly on the shoulder in weak retaliation. Gyllenhal ignored him.

"Eric is a nice guy, I guess, but honestly I only came with him to visit home." Kay seemed to be confessing to them. The fact she was a girl, an attractive female girl at that, talking to them like they were humans, amazed the boys. "Am I a bad person?"

They guys shrugged. Who were they to judge? Or to respond coherently, for that matter.

Kay saw their nervousness and smiled. "So, you think she is cute?" She indicated the woman in the photo.

"Well, yeah," Gyllenhal replied. "Except for the fact that she's dead."

"Who is she?" asked Rosenberg.

"It says that she was found in a peat bog outside of town." She scanned the article with her finger. "Apparently, she is hundreds of years old, but because she was buried in the peat bog, her body is almost perfectly preserved."

"Very, *very* cool!" Gyllenhal said, nodding. Rosenberg nodded along with him.

Kay looked up from the article. "Yes, you should find this interesting because you don't have things like this in your country. They think she might be a witch!"

"Oh we have witches," Rosenberg told her.

Gyllenhal counted off on his fingers. "Yeah, Salem witch trials, the Wicked Witch of the West, Marcie Pillsbury in eighth grade . . ." Rosenberg snickered.

"This one was more like one of your Salem witches. If she was one. During the time of witches, they would execute them, then bury them out in the bogs."

"Sucks for them," said Rosenberg.

"Well, they were witches, doofus."

Kay shrugged. "More likely they were just some people that other people didn't like. And they used superstitions to accuse people they didn't like of witchcraft. And they killed them."

"See, I told you it sucked for them."

Kay went on. "If you do believe in such things, though, you might believe what others believed."

"Like what?"

"That since they weren't buried on consecrated ground, their souls were in constant torment and agony, and would often walk the earth."

Kay smiled. Then she folded the newspaper and handed it to Gyllenhal.

"I'll translate the rest of it later, if you wish. Now I must go to meet my brother."

"Hey, I heard about that," Rosenberg said. "Isn't he sick or something?"

Sheepishly, Kay shook her head No.

"Don't worry," Gyllenhal assured her. "We won't tell."

"Thank you, Ben. And thank you, Pete." She rose to leave.

"Before you go, could you help us?" Gyllenhal asked. "We're trying to find this address and, um, we got turned around and don't know where to go."

Kay received the slip of paper with the band's address scrawled on it.

"Yes. I will walk you there. It is on my way."

"Oh dude, thanks!" Rosenberg nearly melted with relief.

Kay handed the piece of paper back to Gyllenhal and smiled.

"The Playaz, huh? I hope Cameron likes his ears to bleed."

15

The Playaz were a five-piece, black-clad, Gothic speed-punk band with enough piercings between them to set off airport metal detectors. They all apparently lived together in a one-room flat. Rosenberg and Gyllenhal discussed the booking with the smelly, goateed and multiply-pierced bandleader, Jan, in stilted, clichéd French accents borrowed from old Pink Panther movies. Jan, as well as the rest of the band, knew English perfectly well, but pretended not to, as they often did for their amusement when faced with obviously hapless Americans.

After the pair had gone, Jan opened the envelope given to him, and by the size of the check knew right away the dude up in the castle, hapless or not, was at least rich. But the envelope contained a note clipped to yet another piece of paper that, in some ways, he found more interesting than the check itself.

* * *

"You've been quiet all morning," Cameron said to Sofia. They had walked the gardens, the ones on the side of the castle opposite of their tower. Cameron had made sure of that. The day was bright, though crisp. And despite the near-winter weather, bright red and white daisies bloomed all around them. Fresh mulch underneath indicated the flowers had been freshly planted, and could have come from any greenhouse in the world, despite being out of season here. The flowers wouldn't last long. But then, they weren't meant to.

"I keep . . . remembering things," Sofia finally said.

Cameron tensed.

"Like what?"

"About this girl, Ophelia. And how sad and angry she is. And how hurt she was."

"Because of this Hamlet?"

"Because of Hamlet, yeah, but not just hurt by him. By her father, her brother, just about everyone around her. From what I could tell, she got a raw deal. I think something terrible happened to her. And really none of it was her fault." She paused for a while and seemed to contemplate a nearby flower. Cameron didn't interrupt her.

"Well, I would never hurt you," He encircled her with her arms, meaning to kiss her, but she pulled away.

"Look," she snapped. "I told you already. I'm only here because this is a free trip. It doesn't mean you're 'getting any.'" She vulgarly thrust her hips forward to emphasize the point. "Not from me at least!"

Cameron was stunned.

Sofia's lashes fluttered, her eyes turning slightly up into her head, as if she were about to have an epileptic seizure. Then she was back, disoriented for a moment.

"Where was I?" she said, then shrugged off the sudden cobwebs. "I know you wouldn't hurt me, Cameron."

She put her arm back around his and they continued their walk. It then became Cameron's turn to be silent for a while.

The atmosphere of Castle Elsinore was charged with activity. In the kitchens, the staff were busily preparing food for Cameron's party. Elsewhere, housekeeping had failed to locate Frieda or her housekeeping cart. The head housekeeper figured she had been "distracted" by one of the young, handsome guests. A girl that attractive, explained the toadlike old career housekeeper, always got into "that" kind of trouble, and wondered aloud, and rather melodramatically, why she hired a girl like "that." Some of the plainer girls on staff secretly wished one day to be "that" kind of girl, but for now were content with the job security their generic looks apparently ensured.

Anyone seeing the errant girl was to inform her immediately to leave the premises, ordered the head housekeeper.

Immediately *after* she disclosed the whereabouts of the laundry cart, which was of much more long-term concern.

A room to room search would be conducted, but after the guests had departed in order to cause the least fuss. Besides, with the young Americans tramping all over the castle, no doubt someone would stumble upon the cart sooner rather than later, saving them all the trouble of looking.

And indeed, the guests were more than making themselves at home within the walls and on the grounds of Castle Elsinore. The age and beauty of the place, the grandiosity of its design and luxury of its furnishings, made most of the guests feel like they were staying in a museum. Even those least inclined to be impressed by history and beauty were inspired to explore at least part of the castle or its grounds, if only to find privacy. And privacy wasn't that difficult to find. The estate of Castle Elsinore was so large that couples rarely strayed across each other. This was both convenient for them, and deadly dangerous as Ophelia encountered them and murdered them, two by two.

When Frieda and Maddy's melancholy euphoria wore off, Ophelia realized that for the time being, it was important to conceal her presence and her deeds. Discovery would cause panic and likely lead to Cameron leaving before she had become powerful enough to overcome Sofia's spirit. And so she had descended into a girl she came to know as Atara, as she and her boyfriend admired the view from the cliffs facing Sweden. From their appearance, Ophelia assumed the two were noble-born Moors. Once inside, Ophelia/Atara found they were both from a place known as "Philly." They would never return to this place; Ophelia insured that as she wrapped Ty in an inescapable bear hug that he initially thought was romantic roughhousing. His perspective changed as she leapt out over the cliff, still holding him. Ophelia rose out of Atara just before the couple slammed into a shallow part of the ocean right between two similarly tall, widely spaced rocks.

The impact on the jagged rocks just below the surface made drowning irrelevant. No one would find these two.

Hovering there, the first wave of sadness hit Ophelia. She was prepared for it, anxious for it now. She pulsed with the shattered hopes of the couple she had just murdered. And she felt fine.

Then came the riptide pull of the euphoria.

"Time to get my *groove* on!" Ophelia cried to herself in yet another new and exciting dialect.

16

Cameron walked an increasingly addled Sofia back to their room. From the moment of her outburst, she alternated between her own personality and someone else's. From what he could tell, more than one personality was involved. Her statements, while directed at him, didn't relate to him or their relationship in the least. Her mind seemed like a car radio scanning station signals. It would lock on one, there'd be a few seconds of anger and jealousy, then she would be herself again until she locked into another wave of someone else's emotions. All the while, she seemed not to realize what she was doing. Despite her ignorance of her behavior, it was having a physical effect on her. She rapidly became exhausted, and began having trouble holding a thought.

After he tucked her into bed for a nap, he shut the balcony doors to seal out as much as he could the sound of waves crashing upon the nearby rocks.

Whether this helped her to sleep, he didn't know. It calmed his nerves, though.

What was happening to her? he wondered. Since last night, Sofia seemed to be unraveling. This loss of control, these intruding personalities, were antithetical to the Sofia he loved.

Now what would he do?

Tomorrow, he thought. *It's all about tomorrow.* If she's still acting strange tomorrow, then he'll spare no expense to find out what's wrong and to help her.

He clung to that thought. This inheritance would solve all his problems: past, present and future.

Walking into the bathroom, he ran some cool water and splashed his face. His lack of sleep was weighing on him, but he couldn't afford to rest now. He needed to make sure that Rosenberg and Gyllenhal had delivered the envelope to The Playaz. As he dried his face on a towel, his nose caught a faint scent in the air.

Dead lilacs.

Aunt Claudia.

She had been in their room while they were out! He walked back into the bedroom, closed his eyes and focused. No, he couldn't smell anything here, but then, the room was bigger and the balcony doors had been open when they returned. The scent wouldn't have lingered for more than a few seconds. But returning to the bathroom, large to be sure, but much smaller than the bedroom and without a moving breeze, her cologne wouldn't have dissipated as quickly. And it didn't.

She'd been caught.

But the question was, why was she there? What was she looking for?

And most important, what did she find?

He ran to the double doors and rushed out onto the balcony. Below, the bushes appeared to be undisturbed. He and Harry had "fluffed" them after disposing of Dr. Paulsen's body, bending the branches back upon their breaks, making them look whole. Only pushing them down physically would reveal the breaks.

Running from the room, he wound his way through the castle in order to inspect them.

He passed Rosenberg and Gyllenhal in the main foyer. He barely stopped long enough for them to say they had delivered the envelope as planned. Cameron thanked them as he ran off.

Finally, he made it to the base of the tower. Peering down into the bushes, he could see that one branch had been bent back, revealing the break. But was this the result of wind, or had someone been searching the bushes? His heart began to race and he ran toward the garden shed. He threw open the sliding door, ignoring the seagull screech, and saw immediately that the wheelbarrow stood where he and Harry had left it.

Cameron turned from the shed, not noticing that another item was missing. He was thinking of his aunt. Sure, she had been in his room, but what could she have found? He seemed reasonably sure that there was nothing to find. The branch, he decided, was bent due to the wind. It was nothing that would cause any concern unless someone really started pulling on the branches.

Okay, so she didn't know about Dr. Paulsen. Probably. But she *had* entered their room without his permission.

And he was going to take care of that right now.

Twenty-five minutes, two wrong turns and one wrong door later, Cameron arrived at the door to the Queen's Chamber. His mother's feeble voice called for him to answer when he knocked on the door.

He flew to her side immediately upon entering. She struggled to sit up in bed, still wearing her nightgown, even though it was now early afternoon. Her skin was parchment paper, brittle and yellow-white.

"Mom, what's wrong?" She had been bedridden for a week after his father's death. As he did then, he knelt beside her bed and took her hand.

"I just can't cope, Cam. I just can't." She shook her head, on the verge of tears.

"With what?" Anger rose up and squeezed out of his narrowed eyes. "Did Claudia hurt you? I'll kill her if—"

Geri squeezed her son's hand and shook her head. "No, no. No more killing."

"So she does know," he said, fear settling down on him.

"Yes, she knows," Geri said. And by her face, Cameron could see that it was true.

"She was in our room today while we were out," he told her.

"Claudia came to warn you," Geri said. "You should have seen the look in her eyes. I haven't seen that look since . . ." She let her voice trail off, as if the memory of the last time she had seen that certain look in Claudia's face, and its aftermath, was too much to bear.

"You've got to stop it, Cam. Or something terrible will happen."

"Something terrible has already happened, Mother." He was talking about Dr. Paulsen. He was about to explain it all, resting the accident squarely on his shoulders, when his mother said a curious thing.

"Yes, something terrible has happened. And you've made it quite clear to Claudia that you think she's responsible."

"Huh?"

"The gifts, Cam. The chocolate turtles, the necklace with the lizard on it." She reached out to him, imploring him to come near. "If you persist in taunting her this way . . . I don't know what she'll do."

Cameron looked at his mother's face. She obviously knew nothing about Dr. Paulsen, but her expression did nothing to quell the anger raging in him. The sight of her in bed, frail and dewey-eyed evoked not tenderness, but revulsion.

"I don't want you to get hurt, Cam, honey," his mother said in a doll's voice.

"You don't want *me* to get hurt?" he said, his voice rising to a shout. "You don't want *me* hurt?! What about *Dad*? Was it okay for him to get hurt?" He was bellowing now, looming above her in bed. She shrunk away from him. She was weeping now.

"You don't know what she's capable of."

"Oh, I think I know what good old Aunt Claudia's capable of, Mom," he said, lowering his voice. "Isn't that the point of this little conversation?" With lightning reflexes, he grabbed her wrist and pulled her face up to his. "Or do you mean what she's capable of in bed?" he hissed. "I don't *even* want to think about that."

Geri struggled against her son, but could not break his grip. She turned away and tried to slip out the other side of the bed, but Cameron yanked her toward him. She toppled onto the floor at his feet.

"Cameron! Stop!"

"Oh, you like it rough, do you? Is that how Aunt Claudia is?" He mimicked her panicked whine. "'Oh Claudia, stop! Don't! Stop! Don't stop! DON'T STOP!!'" He was practically screaming. Geri dissolved into sobs on the stone floor of the chamber, one hand in the air still held tightly by Cameron.

"What are *you* capable of, Mom?"

He let go of her arm and his mother collapsed completely to the floor. Moments later, he lay facing his mother, who had begun to curl up into a fetal position. He studied her for a moment as she sobbed. Beneath the ruin of her face, he could see the pretty woman she had once been. In the frailty of her limbs, he could see the delicacy they had once possessed. And as for her breasts, which even now threatened to spill from her tangled nightgown, they retained an inviting shape that no amount of plastic surgery could have duplicated.

Gently, Cameron lifted a lock of hair away from his mother's eyes. She recoiled at his touch, like a feral creature, but he held her firmly in place.

Quietly, he said to her, "What *are* you capable of, Mother? Isn't that a fair question? You lie in bed, with and without my father, with and without Aunt Claudia. The world turns around you, people live and people die, and you just can't seem to get yourself out of bed to cope. All the money I'm about to inherit tomorrow couldn't buy me that kind of luxury."

He kissed her gently on the forehead and stood. With one arm, he swept the blankets out of the way, then stooped and took his mother into his arms. Her body radiated heat with fever intensity. Nonetheless, she shivered as he set her on the bed and covered her with the blankets.

"I won't be angry with you if don't come down for the party," he told her. "It'll be a loud party. I know you don't like loud parties."

And he left.

Lounging in the drowning body of the girl she had just possessed, Ophelia luxuriated. The power of shadow love coursed through her. Oblivious to the impending physical death, she drew the blankets, soaked with swamp water and blood, to her dribbling chin.

This had been her favorite pair yet. Two souls, in near-perfect harmony, yet hiding their joy from others they professed to love. Cheaters, in other words. Shadow lovers.

Ophelia had discovered them in one of the rooms of a closed-off wing, far from the inhabited areas. Their light glowed with a hue the ghost had not yet encountered.

She had found the couple naked, the boy lying on his back and the girl upright, sitting astride him. The girl stared at the ceiling; the boy's eyes were closed.

The sensation she experienced dropping into the girl's body was startling. He was inside her. For the first time since her first accidental possession, Ophelia panicked. She tore the girls eyes from the ceiling and looked down at the boy who had just begun to sense a change. Ophelia screamed through the girl's mouth, a strangled gargling that ejected a gout of stagnant water into the boy's face. Quickly, she trapped his arms against his body and squeezed with her legs. He was immobilized, and a second squeeze forced the breath from his body. Ribs cracked beneath her. He could only wheeze his terror.

And then she tore his head off.

There was a crackle of vertebrae, then a tearing sound. With that she rolled off the boy and onto her back, relieved to have stopped the boy's invasion of the girl's body. Of her body.

Then the waves hit her, a sadness made even more delicious by the girl's need to hide her unfaithfulness. She had loved another one, one with whom she was still paired, but her desire for the boy in this room had been more invigorating and more complete. Her shadow lover had been ready to reveal their relationship. He had made an ultimatum: him or me. That had terrified her.

They made love while she considered an answer.

Ophelia contemplated the boy's face as she held his head up before her. Feeling the body she inhabited slipping from her, she tossed the head away.

The last thing she thought as the girl's body shuddered and died was that she needed a smoke.

A being with perceptions similar to Ophelia's would have seen her pulsating, rippling with colors as she hovered in the room. Even a human walking past the door would have noticed light dancing from underneath, like a reflection from a swimming pool at night.

Yes, Ophelia thought, *Sofia had been delicious.*

As she waited for the ecstasy to take her, she suddenly realized that it had not been Sofia that she had just killed. The girl's name had been ...

What *had* the girl's name been?

For the first time, Ophelia could not remember. She had retained memories, sensations and feelings, clearly drawn from this girl. But only the identity of Sofia remained in her mind.

Then it hit. And Ophelia rose upward on the wave of ecstasy. Yes, she was close, now. Close to being able to overcome Sofia. Ready to experience the love she had once been denied. Soon, she and Cameron would be married.

Ophelia faltered, suddenly disoriented.

No.

Hamlet. It was Hamlet she would be united with. Hamlet. Whom she hated and loved.

Hamlet who? She suddenly found herself asking. *Cam's my man.*

Then, she was Ophelia once more. Soon, Sofia would be dead, Cameron would be dead and Hamlet would be hers for eternity.

Ophelia's need for secrecy was nearly at an end. When she had become powerful enough to take Sofia, no one would be able to stop her from her goal.

So tonight would be the night. She would share her triumph with the remaining souls in this place.

The celebration she now knew was planned for the evening would be perfect.

She would deliver a final round of vengeance upon the hapless mortals infesting the place, reveal her angry presence, then take her due.

Ophelia's body began to glitter again, this time in anticipation of what she would achieve tonight. She floated this way for quite some time, for once not looking for prey. There would plenty for later.

Because, she thought, *tonight we're gonna party like it's 1349.*

17

Castle Elsinore was alive tonight, its beating heart a bank of speakers on the north side of the courtyard that pumped out a constant electronic bass line.

A Danish DJ stood on a metal stage set up in front of the speakers. Before him was an array of turntables, CD players, other equipment and a complicated mixing board that took the energy of a small city to power and looked like a missile silo control panel. Shaggy, dyed-black hair stuck at odd angles from beneath a large set of earphones that looked more natural on him than ears themselves. Light reflected off mirror lenses. The DJ was one with the equipment, not just manipulating it. His head bobbed to the beat he was about to unleash upon the gathering, each hand dancing from knob to lever independent of the other, seemingly independent of the DJ's head.

Smoke machines, strobe lights and lasers, all part of the musical organism, filled the castle courtyard with atmosphere and potential carcinogens. The hardcore ravers among the group had already found the dance floor before the stage, heads bobbing in hive-mind thrall.

The food and drink table stood at the south end of the courtyard. Tiki torches waged a losing battle with the lasers and strobes invading from the north. Just reaching for a canapé was a disorienting experience. Light reflecting off each background, object and person seemed to shift in random, unmotivated intervals, changing the perceived distance of every detail from moment to moment. Tables seemed to rock from side to side, the food upon it attempting to dodge the hand reaching for it.

Cameron had promised a rager and had delivered a rager. And the night had only begun.

"Where is everyone?" Cameron wondered aloud. He scanned the courtyard. At the moment, the staff outnumbered the guests. Besides the ravers, there were only a few other clumps of guests scattered about the courtyard. He and Sofia stood by the food table, filling plastic cups with beer from the keg.

"Don't worry," Sofia told him. "You know how people are fashionably late."

They clinked cups together and sipped in silence for a moment. Cameron stared at Sofia from behind his beer.

"Don't look at me like that!" Sofia said suddenly. "I'm fine."

"Are you sure?"

"Ask me that one more time and I'm gonna head-butt you!" She was only partially kidding.

Ever since she awoke from her nap, he had been treating her as if she would suddenly sprout wings and fly away. She was aware of having felt poorly earlier, perhaps having had another blackout. But the sleep had cleared her head miraculously, and she had told Cameron so. Besides, she didn't want to dwell on the negative, or the possibilities that something might be wrong with her. So, she didn't tell Cameron about the dreams: the sadness, the confusion, the hopelessness.

The drowning.

She had startled awake when the girl featured in her dream had looked up from the bottom of the swamp in which she had thrown herself. Seaweed tangled in her hair, entwined with her limbs. The girl's last act had been to reach up for the flowers she had been obsessively sorting and naming in her dementia. They now floated on the water's surface, the bright sunlight cutting through the murk of the swamp water. The flowers danced as fairies above her head. She wanted to touch them.

But the water filled her lungs and Sofia awoke choking. She could taste the rot in her mouth and nearly vomited. Luckily, Cameron had not returned from seeing his mother, or she would really deserve the cautious looks he was giving her.

When he *did* return, Cameron himself seemed distracted and did not notice the last vestiges that remained of her spell. A quick shower dissolved the last of it, and by the time she had finished, even Cameron had returned to normal. But as the night wore on, his concern increased to obsession. She forgave him; likely he was projecting his own nervousness of the momentousness of his birthday this year. At midnight, he would become twenty-one and an insanely rich young man. He would want for nothing for the rest of his life.

For the rest of *their* life, she reminded herself.

Even she felt the intensity. No wonder he had become more manic as the party approached.

But that didn't make his asking if she were all right any less annoying.

"Where's Harry? He was supposed to meet us down here twenty minutes ago." Cameron had begun to pace.

She grabbed him by the shoulder to stop him.

"Just calm down, birthday boy!" He tried to pull away from her but she wouldn't let him. "At least you've seen him today. I haven't seen my father or my brother since last night."

"Isn't that a good thing?" he said, drowning his distress in a gulp of beer.

"Usually," she agreed, "But I'm serious about making peace with him, pronto."

Cameron examined the bottom of his cup, pretending to look for a bug that might have drowned. It was the best he could do to hide the shame of what he knew, of what he had done. It was either that or run screaming.

Cameron surveyed the room again. The staff still outnumbered the guests.

"Stop doing that!" Sofia scolded. "You'll just freak yourself out even more."

Cameron took a deep breath. She was right, even if she didn't know all the reasons why.

"Hey, Cam! Hey, Sofia!" Rosenberg and Gyllenhal sidled up to them at the food table in all their preppy Banana Republic splendor. Rosenberg raised his hand to Cameron for a high five. "What it *is*?"

Cameron frowned and high-fived him back.

"Looking good, Cam," Gyllenhal told him, giving Cameron's jeans and polo shirt a once-over.

Rosenberg's eyes danced over Sofia. "You too, Sofia. That blouse is fantastic!"

"Thanks, guys," Sofia told him. "I gotta say, you guys are looking pretty good, too."

And that was the weird part. It might have been the lighting, but Sofia noticed that their khakis fit better than she had ever noticed. Rosenberg's shirt was open at the collar one buttonhole lower than usual. Gyllenhal's shoulders seemed broader, filling out the knit pullover he was wearing. All the while they had been on the football team, she had never thought of them as athletes. Or possessing athletic physiques.

She frowned at them—at herself, really—surprised at her sudden appreciation for two guys she had always considered geeks. It was like finding out her little brother had had sex. And to her knowledge, Larry had done nothing of the sort.

"Something wrong, honey?" Cameron asked.

"No," she said, shaking off the unbidden image of what would be revealed if Rosenberg undid just one more button. "Need more beer."

"Not too fast," he told her. "It's early."

"Anyways, guys," Gyllenhal told him, looking around the courtyard. "Ben and I are gonna check out the hedge maze before the party kicks up."

"You're not gonna hang at the party?" Cameron asked. Finally, friends had arrived and they were already leaving.

"Hey, don't worry, Cam," Gyllenhal told him. "You're gonna be playing host, so we won't be able to hang with you long, and it's not like we're gonna be scoring chicks here tonight."

"Yeah, the problem with parties where you pretty much know everyone," Rosenberg added.

"So we just thought we'd do some exploring before things really take off."

"It'll be cool, Cam," Rosenberg said, slapping him on his shoulder. "We'll be back long before midnight. Wouldn't come all this way, on your dime, and dis you on your birthday."

"Right," Gyllenhal agreed. "See you guys later. Bye Sofia."

"Later," Sofia replied as the two took off. She and Cameron watched them in silence as they left the courtyard.

"Did you notice anything different about them?" Sofia asked.

Cameron shook his head. "Not really. Why?"

"Well, this is gonna sound weird, and I don't know how this happened, but Rosenberg and Gyllenhal are sexy!"

Cameron nearly choked on his beer.

"I hope you're happy!" Claudia's voice slammed like a wrecking ball through the din. Suddenly, she was beside them, arms crossed and foot tapping. Her gray pants suit made her look like a prison matron and her hair was pulled so tightly back in a bun that her face could have been springloaded. Dead lilac drifted from her like sugary sweat. That immediately set Cameron on edge. He barely noticed the prescription bottle she held in one hand.

"Your mother is a wreck!"

"Cameron!" Sofia said sharply.

He turned to his girlfriend. "She's exaggerating."

"Oh, am I?" Claudia snarled. "She can't even get out of bed."

Cameron shrugged. "It's her hobby. What can I say?"

"Get over here, buster." Claudia suddenly latched

her claw onto Cameron's arm and pulled him away with greater strength than he would have expected from such a thin woman.

"Let go, I'm coming," he said, finally shrugging her off. They went to an alcove on one side of the courtyard.

"Stop fucking with me, buddy," Claudia snarled. Her face was a mask of pure, unadorned hate. "Whatever you think you know, you better back off, before there's another accident." She paused slightly before the word "accident."

"What do you have planned for me, huh, Aunt *Claud?*" The nickname made her wince. "Gonna stuff a toad full of blowfish venom and afflict me with lethal warts?"

The comment hit home. He could see the corner of her left eyelid twitch.

"Listen to me," she seethed. "Midnight doesn't come for another couple of hours. And lots can happen between now and then to come between a certain brat and his inheritance. So watch yourself."

They stared at each other for a minute, neither wanting to back down. Finally, it was Claudia who surrendered.

"Here," she said, handing him the pill vial she had been holding. "Watch your friends, too."

"What is it?" he said, shaking it. Pills rattled within.

"The boy told me it was Ecstasy," she said. Cameron looked inside and didn't recognize the pill. He'd never used X.

"So why are you giving this to me?" he asked.

"As a warning. Being party to drug use at your *current* age is *just* the kind of thing that could be used to prove one is unworthy and unfit to inherit such a large estate. A hearing, should such allegations come to light, could at the very least delay your windfall for quite some time, even if you were ultimately found not responsible." She was in his face now, her dead lilac scent almost stifling. "So you'll want to make sure your friends don't fuck things up for you. And you'll be helping me, too."

"How?" he asked, suspicious.

"Because I want to be the one who brings you down. No one else gets that privilege." Despite the dead calm of her statement, the corner of her eye still twitched. She stalked away to a vantage point at the opposite end of the food table, near the punch bowls.

* * *

Cameron returned to Sofia's side. She handed him a fresh beer.

"What was that all about?"

"More family crap I don't want to bother you with," he told her.

"Uh-uh," she told him. "If we're getting married, if we're gonna be a family, you can't do that."

He thought about it for a moment, then sighed. "Okay, from now on. But will you give this one a 'bye?' Please?"

She frowned, but then nodded. "Fine, but from now on, we share all our family's problems."

He clinked her cup. "Here's hoping there won't be any after tonight," he said.

18

Nearly an hour later, the courtyard had started to fill up. Still, there were notable absences among the crowd. At the moment, Cameron was only worried about Harry, who still had not shown up. Neither had Larry. Of course, Dr. Paulsen wasn't due to make an appearance, probably never would again if the currents had their way, but Sofia didn't know that.

"Let's go look for him," he finally told Sofia.

Behind the DJ, the band was beginning to set up.

"Tell you what," Sofia told him. "You go get Harry and Shayne. I'm going to find out what's keeping Larry and my dad."

"Okay," he agreed. He looked around to see where Claudia was. He wanted her in the courtyard, too. He had a special treat for her. He could see her lurking near the punch bowls, in the tiki flame shadows. It occurred to him that she could lurk on a beach at noon.

Since their confrontation, she had pretty much stayed put, drinking punch and seeming content to watch the proceedings. *Good,* he thought. She seemed likely to stick around.

But Harry was the missing ingredient. The Playaz were about to go on and he needed Harry to witness their performance. Just then, Harry appeared. His expression was ragged with worry.

"Something's up with Harry," Cameron said to Sofia.

"You go take care of him, I'm still going to hunt down Larry and Dad."

"Okey-doke."

Letting her go, he crossed over to Harry.

"Where's Shayne?" he asked.

"Shayne's gone. She went for a walk this afternoon and never came back!"

Out in the hedge maze, Rosenberg and Gyllenhal were completely lost. Finding the center of the maze had been easy. But somehow, the way out eluded them.

"If I die first," Gyllenhal said as they stood before a dead end that looked exactly like the last one that had faced them, "you have my permission to eat my body to survive."

"Gee, thanks," said Rosenberg. They turned and headed down another passageway. "Same for you, then."

The hedges rose high above their heads. As solid as the bushes were, they wouldn't support weight, so climbing on top to get their bearings was not an option.

"Hey, what's that?"

Rosenberg pointed at a discoloration in the uniform green of the foliage—a patch of brown and dark green slime on the wall to their left. Dead leaves not belonging to hedge shrubs mingled with the muck. Gyllenhal picked at it.

"Strange. This looks like the stuff I pulled off of you in the castle the other day."

Rosenberg leaned in and gave it a sniff.

"Gross."

"Well, don't smell it, ya moron!"

Rosenberg stepped back and looked at the patch, which rose about four and a half feet tall in front of them.

"Now that's weird," he said, pointing again.

"It's kinda shaped like a person, like a silhouette."

Not much longer, Claudia thought with dark glee. By now, the party was in full gear. Even the staff seemed to be enthralled by the lights and music, barely paying attention to their duties, or to any one individual.

I could walk in here with a bazooka, she thought. *No one would even notice until after, say, the third shot. And they'd only hear* that *if the DJ played a slow song.*

But she didn't need a bazooka. And if she did, by tomorrow, she'd be able to afford all the bazookas she needed.

Cameron had pulled Harry over to the keg.

"We're almost there, Harry," Cameron said in a low voice. "We gotta focus. I need your help."

"Shayne's been gone for hours." He ran his fingers through his hair absently. Cameron thrust a beer into his friend's free hand.

"I'm sure she's fine. She's probably in the library or something. This is a historical candy store for someone like her. She probably just lost track of time. It's easy here because the light rarely changes."

Harry took a contemplative chug from his cup.

"Okay, whatever." Then he emptied the cup and began to refill it. "So what's gonna happen?"

"Just pay attention to when the band goes on. I wrote them a 'special' song. You'll know it when you hear it. And when you do, keep an eye on my aunt."

"Then what?" asked Harry. "Even if that proves it to you and me, there's still no proof you could supply to a court."

"I won't need to!" Cameron said. "She's close. Look at her." He tilted his head slightly in her direction. She stood examining the crowd, tapping her nail file absently against the side of her cup. "Her eye's twitching. She even threatened me. She's close to breaking. She'll either break down and admit what she's done—"

"*Tell-Tale Heart*," Harry said. Plagued by the phantom sound of a murder victim's beating heart, the murderer confessed, raving mad with guilt. Cameron's gifts had been meant to produce that same effect.

"Yeah. Or she'll try something with me," Cameron finished. "Either way, she's got to make a move soon. If she waits until midnight, when I turn twenty-one, it'll be too late."

For the first time since he entered the courtyard, Harry focused completely on his friend.

"But Cam, if your aunt tries something, don't you think it will be to bump you off?"

Cameron shook his head emphatically. "Nope. Too many people around. She'd never get away with it. I think she just wants to set up a situation that makes me seem unfit, like mentally unstable or something, so she can retain control of the inheritance. She said as much herself."

"Gee, Cam," Harry said. "Let's see: You're trying to prove your aunt murdered your father, with a turtle no less, by driving her crazy, *and* hiding the accidental death of your fiance's father because you don't want to hurt her feelings." He snorted a bitter laugh. "Yeah, she's got nothing on you."

"Have faith, bro," Cameron said, laying a hand on

his friend's shoulder. "When I call the play, I win the game. Trust me."

On the way to her father's room, Sofia stumbled. Something was wrong. She had the sensation of flying out of her body. Suddenly, from an impossible vantage point she was looking down upon the courtyard. Far below her, scattered groups of guests drank, talked, and laughed. The dance floor was filled with bodies pulsating like platelets in a bloodstream. Cameron's aunt Claudia stood smiling to herself near the punch. Finally, Cameron and Harry came into view, conferring secretively near the keg. And it all seemed wrong.

Strangely, she had the feeling she was looking for herself. And not finding herself made her angry.

Then, her consciousness returned to the mansion, to her body lying on the cold stone floor of a back hallway, where she had fainted. Using a railing above her, she pulled herself unsteadily to her feet. Instead of going to her father's room, she returned to her own; she had to lie down.

A feeling of impending disaster grew within her. She felt like someone who could tell a big storm was coming because of a bunion. The bigger the storm, the greater the bunion throbbed. Had that been the case now, her bunion would have exploded and shattered her entire leg.

* * *

In the distance, speaker feedback squawked.

"Shit, the band's going on," Gyllenhal said. "We gotta get back."

They had just found another strange muck patch. According to what they could tell, the patches appeared on opposite sides of the same hedge, as if something had passed through the hedge. Something the size of a small person. Tracking down more patches had nearly distracted them from leaving the maze entirely.

While Gyllenhal contemplated this one, and worried about making it back to the party, Rosenberg continued around the corner to see if the patch went through to the other side.

A moment later, Rosenberg yelped. A thud indicated that he had fallen.

"Ben?"

Gyllenhal dashed around the corner and tripped as well. On the dead body that lay across the path. He landed facedown on Rosenberg, who had rolled onto his back.

"Ack!" Rosenberg cried, the wind suddenly knocked out of him.

Ahead of them, Gyllenhal could see what at first looked like a pile of laundry with a Globe jacket on top. Then his mind adjusted, quite unwillingly, to the concept that it was another corpse. Even from his low angle atop Rosenberg he could tell the guy's back was bent in an impossible angle.

"Did you see? That's Marc over there!" Gyllenhal was so panicked, he didn't even move. His face was inches from Rosenberg's.

"Yeah, I saw," Rosenberg wheezed, trying to gulp in breaths. "What're we gonna do?"

"Oh, God, I don't know, I don't know!" Gyllenhal sunk his face into his friend's shoulder.

"Hey!" Rosenberg said suddenly. "Get off!" He heaved Gyllenhal to the side and sat up. "We gotta do something."

Gyllenhal rolled over and sat up too. Then he scuttled backward—his legs were touching the body of the girl he now recognized as Carla.

They stood.

"Look, she's covered with the same guck," Rosenberg pointed out. Above her was another patch in the shrubs. A second one appeared in the hedge a few feet past Marc's body. Gyllenhal swallowed and reached down to turn her over.

"Don't." Rosenberg had grabbed his arm to stop him. Gyllenhal stepped back from the body.

They went over to Marc's corpse. He lay on his side, folded like a lawn chair. Rosenberg barfed.

"What the hell happened to him?" he said when he could speak again.

"Come on, Ben," Gyllenhal said. "We gotta get out of here and tell someone. Cam'll call the police or something."

Gyllenhal helped Rosenberg stand, they stepped

carefully around Marc, then took off running.

Two turns later, they ran into another dead end.

"Shit!" Gyllenhal shouted. "Back that way."

"Hey!!" Rosenberg suddenly shouted into the sky. "Help! Help us!"

Gyllenhal shook his head.

"That's no use," he said. And he was right: in the distance, The Playaz had begun to play.

19

At about the time Rosenberg and Gyllenhal were pondering the mystery of the muck patches, the DJ in the courtyard faded the music down. The lasers and strobes winked out as well, leaving only the green glow of the now-stationary stage lights. Leaning down at the mike, the DJ's expression looked more like he was examining a bug crawling across his instruments than preparing to address the crowd.

"Howdy, Globe University," he said in an affected monotone.

There were a few hoots and cheers in response from the crowd.

"The band's up next, but before they go on, let's bring up our host, the birthday boy—Cameron Dean." He raised his head, still cocked at its deliberately curious angle, meeting the crowd with a thin-lipped smile.

Applause rose from the dance floor and cheers broke out all over the courtyard. All eyes turned to

Cameron, who was to the left of the stage, talking with Jan of The Playaz. Cameron looked up and had to take a moment to shake off his deer-caught-in-the-headlights look. He swapped a quick glance with Harry, who nodded grimly. As the applause raged on, Cameron slapped on a smile and went up onto the stage. The DJ handed him the mike.

"Hey, everyone!" Though his voice boomed from the speakers, the crowd managed to drown it out. He paused, waiting for it to die down. Raising his hands, he gestured for them to let him speak. Finally, he only faced a few scattered whoops.

"All right, cool," he said, stepping forward. A loud screech of feedback zapped the crowd. The DJ pulled him backward a couple of steps and he continued.

"Everyone having fun?" he shouted. The crowd went nuts again, but quickly settled back down. "Excellent. Well, it's almost time. In a little over an hour, I'll be twenty-one. And officially"—he looked pointedly at Claudia—"the proud owner of this castle."

"Dude that rocks!" Pierson shouted from the back of the crowd.

"Yeah, but I just want everyone to know, it means a lot that you guys are here."

A melodramatic "Awww!" rose from the dance floor.

"Seriously now, guys," Cameron lowered his voice. "I'm just bummed that my father isn't here." He fell silent, and so did the crowd. Several seconds later, he raised his head and smiled. "Didn't wanna be a downer, just wanted to take a moment. Anyway, I'm done here. The Playaz are gonna shift gears and I'll consider this party a huge success if we've torn the castle down by morning!"

Cheers and whistles rose in the courtyard for the last time that evening before the screaming began. The Playaz took the stage as Cameron handed Jan the microphone. Cameron winked. Jan smiled and nodded back.

"Hello, you lousy Americans!" Jan snarled into the mike, then let loose with an earsplitting guitar chord. The crowd ate it up. "No, you suck! You really do! Lemme tell you how much in this first song." He sneered at the crowd and croaked out, "Yankee Go Homo!"

With that, The Playaz launched into a sonic anti-American diatribe that couldn't have charmed the crowd more quickly and completely. The single-minded, pulsating hive creature re-formed on the dance floor again. This time, however, the mood was frantic, desperate, verging on violence. The creature was on the attack.

A half hour later, Rosenberg and Gyllenhal finally emerged from the maze. It was the far entrance, and they had to run back along one side of the maze to return to the courtyard. Both were out of breath, but stopping never occurred to them.

"And now, we've got a new song," Jan announced from the stage. They had just finished the disturbing "Amputee Love Song" that, lyrics aside, sounded suspiciously like their previous three songs.

"Okay, showtime," Cameron told Harry. It had been hard to keep him focused. Shayne had still not arrived. Grabbing Harry's shoulders, Cameron physically turned his friend toward his aunt, who continued to hover at the food table.

"This is dedicated to all the killers out there," Jan announced into the microphone. "And you know who you are!"

Cameron and Harry noticed Aunt Claudia pause just before she was about to plunge a cup into the punch bowl.

"Here it comes," Cameron told Harry.

The Playaz tortured their instruments and sang the following song:

> "I had a daddy
> My mommy was his wife
> He also had a sister
> Who took his life.

> "Daddy's dead
> I got two mommies
> Daddy's dead
> I got two mommies

Daddy's dead
I got two mommies
Daddy's dead
I got two mommies."

Jan bleated out the lyrics like a lamb in the process of being slaughtered. The dance floor was a happy mosh pit, people tuned to the sonic assault of the instruments, rather than lyrics. Even those listening would not have realized that Cameron himself had penned them. The lyrics seemed perfectly appropriate to a group whose previous song featured the line, "Your love has got me stumped."

Cameron and Harry watched Claudia, for whom the lyrics struck a meaningful chord. She had frozen in place, her hand holding a cup just above the punch bowl. Jan screeched on.

"She's in my daddy's house
She's in my daddy's clothes
She's even in my mommy
Like the two of them are hos.

"No one knows she killed him
No one knows but me
I know 'cuz daddy told me
His ghost appeared to me."

Claudia dropped the cup she had been holding. It fell beside the table. White pills that had been concealed in it spilled across the floor at her feet. Later analysis would find that they were cyanide. The vial in Cameron's pocket contained cyanide as well. A stockpile of them would also be discovered among Cameron's luggage, enough to kill everyone in the castle. Twice.

Claudia forgot all of that now. She forgot that she had been planning on lacing the punch with cyanide to kill as many guests as possible. Her plan to make it seem that Cameron had been unstable since his father's death, slipped from her mind. The intricate machinations of arranging for Cameron's suicide, his lovely, dead, fiancée-to-be at his side, while she and his mother wept copiously at the tragedy of youth: it all became obliterated by the sonic abomination on stage, where the lead vocalist had just machine-gunned through the refrain and started his final onslaught.

> "So you see this is a love song
> To my Daddy, Mom and Aunt
> If she thinks she'll get away with it
> I'm here to say she can't.
>
> "I'm here to say she can't
> I'm here to say she can't
> I'm here to say she can't
> **GET READY FOR ME, AUNT!**

"Daddy's dead
I got two mommies—"

Claudia's grip on her nail file caused it to cut into her palms. She barely noticed. She turned abruptly, nearly whirling off balance, righted herself, and marched out of the courtyard.

"Daddy's dead
I got two mommies—"

"There, you see that?" Cameron pointed at his aunt as she disappeared through a doorway.

"Well, I'll be damned, Cam." Harry was astonished. "I think it worked."

"Daddy's dead
I got two mommies—"

Rosenberg and Gyllenhal burst into the courtyard from a south doorway.

"Cam! Cam!" They shouted in tandem.

Cameron turned toward them. He could see them waving their hands, but couldn't make out what they were saying.

"Daddy's dead
I got two—"

Suddenly, a pulsating, coruscating fireball shot through the air above the courtyard. People shielded their heads. It had started to rain. Slime.

The fireball hit the stage, striking Jan's electric guitar. Sparks gushed from the guitar. Jan's hair stood up as he was electrocuted. He fell to the metal stage.

There was barely time for anyone to react as the fireball, growing brighter and brighter, whirled around the stage, plunging into each piece of equipment in turn. Soon, the entire stage was a live wire, electricity coursing through metal and water. The Playaz started screaming in unison, a sound barely distinguishable from their singing, as their instruments sparked and exploded. The fireball struck like intelligent lightning.

Someone in the crowd finally screamed.

"Get 'em offa there!" Pierson yelled and ran onto the stage.

"No!" Cameron cried, but it was too late. Pierson became part of the circuit the moment his foot touched the stage. Soon, he fell also, joining the twitching, burning bodies.

The fireball, having destroyed everyone and everything onstage, finally stopped darting about. It hovered in one place, center stage, giving off light and dripping moisture.

"What the hell is that?" someone yelled.

Despite the destruction it had just caused, it looked beautiful, like a deadly jewel.

The smell of ozone and burning flesh began to waft from the stage. And with it, another odor: methane and decay.

The fireball grew brighter and brighter. Then expanded. Without warning, it exploded in a shower of sparks and energy. An unearthly roar emanated from the stage where the fireball hovered.

What emerged was not a fireball. It was the glowing form of a girl.

She had long, flowing hair, tangled with leaves and mud. Her simple peasant dress was torn and rotted. Her arms stretched out toward the crowd, black talons at the end of delicate hands. But worst of all was her face. Her eyes were black, as were her lips. Slime and brackish water leaked from between them. They curled into an enraged snarl.

With a watery, choked bellow, the specter descended from the stage and floated into the crowd.

20

Ophelia had come to party.

Her spirit was aflame with the energy from her kills, as well as the power she had absorbed from the stage's electrical equipment.

"I'm not just here," she bellowed. "I am *so* here!"

She shot into the body of the girl nearest the stage. Instantly, boils rose on the girl's skin and burst in small puffs of steam. Reaching for the boy next to her, she wrapped her burning hands around his throat. His flesh seared at her touch. His agonized scream was cut short as she snapped his neck backward, severing his spinal cord.

She turned her vessel toward the crowd. Ophelia laughed with the girl's voice. This time fetid gases poured from her mouth.

Horrified onlookers backed away from her, not sure of what they were seeing. A hand grabbed her shoulder and then was gone. A cadaverous-looking man, somewhat older than those around him, had intended to stop her. She could see her own horrible visage in his mirrored glasses. And that he clutched at his scalded hand.

Then everything went dark. The girl's eyes exploded from the expansion of her boiling bodily fluids.

Ophelia rose from the pile of steaming flesh that had been her victim. She was still visible to the naked eye. Now people began to run away. Screaming.

The DJ remained nearby, clutching his scalded hand. She flew toward him, through him. She could not possess him, but in her current state, his blood literally boiled in his veins the moment she passed through him. Vapor rose from his lips as the DJ died.

Then she saw him: Cameron. Her Hamlet.

Cameron and Harry stood stunned as the band was electrocuted onstage in front of everyone. They stared, wide-eyed, at the blazing, horrific apparition.

The specter flew into the girl near the stage, seeming to boil her from the inside. But not before she had practically torn her boyfriend's head off. The DJ died next, flash fried.

Then it had turned toward him.

It had seen him.

Recognized him.

As the creature glided toward him, Harry grabbed his shoulder.

"Cam, we gotta get out of here."

But it was too late. She was before them. Cameron closed his eyes, ready to be boiled alive.

He could feel her heat, like standing in front of a furnace. Goose bumps rose on his skin.

Not this way.

Ophelia regarded Cameron, who steeled himself for his fate.

Killing him this way would not bring Hamlet to her. He could only be killed by the one he loved. Sofia. And that was how it would be. How it must be.

But now she had grown too strong. Even though Sofia was stronger than the others she had possessed, even she would not last long if possessed now. And if Sofia died before she could be used to kill Cameron, then Hamlet would be lost to her.

The courtyard reeked of cooked flesh. Party guests ran in every direction, trying to leave the courtyard, so disoriented by what they saw that some simply ran until they bumped into another object or person, changed directions, then ran until they encountered yet another obstacle.

Plenty of people to expend her excess energy on, Ophelia thought. *Plenty more vengeance to taste.*

She hissed at Hamlet.

"Later, 'gator."

She turned away and plunged into the body of a young staffer named Ingrid who was having an affair with the elderly, and married, Mr. Ginn. The porter was standing nearby at the time, observing chaos with the grim stolidity of a captain sworn to go down with his ship.

And down he went, moments later, at the hands of his possessed mistress.

In her room, Sofia looked up into the mirror. She had been obsessively washing her face for the last half hour. At any point, she expected to find another face staring out at her, with her own face washed down the drain. Each time she looked, however, she found herself looking at her own face. It was pink and wet, but hers nonetheless.

Then a wave of nausea and disorientation washed over her. Now she was certain the change had come.

She whispered the name of her doppelgänger.

"Ophelia!"

Slowly she looked up into the mirror once more. This time, it reflected two faces.

Near the service entrance, a zombified maid appeared to be playing "He loves me, he loves me not" with Mr. Ginn's corpse. She was wrestling with his right arm when the maid choked out a jet of steam and fell over. The service entrance was now blocked by a children's joke: What was black-and-white and red all over? The pile of limbs and blood that had once been a porter and a maid.

The ghost cast an exultant glance toward Cameron and plunged through a wall into the castle.

"Friend of yours?" asked Harry. The ghost's recognition of his friend was inescapable.

"I don't know. But I'm not sticking around to find out."

"Good plan."

A scream from inside the castle floated into the courtyard.

"Sofia!" It wasn't her voice, but he was reminded of the danger she was in nonetheless. "I've got to get her. And my mom."

"Right behind you, buddy," Harry said clapping him on the shoulder. "I'm not leaving without Shayne."

And they dashed into the castle.

Rosenberg and Gyllenhal marched down the hallway, each brandishing a camera as if they were Uzis.

When they saw the ghost burst into the courtyard, they forgot all about the corpses in the hedge maze. When they saw what it had done to the girl near the stage, they forgot about anyone else and hauled ass out of the courtyard.

A herd of people, staff and guests alike, were already running down the long hill toward Kronborg. Rosenberg suddenly stopped short, remembering the cameras in their rooms; one very expensive, both owned by the university.

"We'll get in trouble if we leave them behind," he said and dashed back into the castle.

Gyllenhal followed protesting, until Rosenberg told him of a brainstorm he had. Despite his initial fear, and the fact he was certain that his friend had gone completely nuts, the idea sounded way too cool not to try.

On the way there, they had passed several fleeing guests, but had seen no sign of the ghost. Occasionally a scream or strangled cry would echo from somewhere, but the size of the castle made it difficult to determine a direction.

This had given them time to think out a few things.

"So you noticed that the ghost only went *directly* into the girls," Rosenberg said. "Remember Carla and Marc? She was all slimy and suffocated. He was just . . . broken."

"So, stay away from girls is what you're saying?" Gyllenhal said.

"Well, the ones with the black tongues," Rosenberg shrugged.

Making it to their room without incident, the pair retrieved their cameras. Rosenberg grabbed his Polaroid, Gyllenhal the 35mm Nikon.

Stepping back into the hallway, they ran into the thing they least wanted to see at the moment. A girl.

"Ben, Pete, what is going on here?" It was Kay.

"I think it's a ghost," Gyllenhal told her. "I mean, what else could it be?"

Kay then noticed they were holding cameras. "What are you doing? You should run."

Rosenberg and Gyllenhal shared a dramatic, secret smile, then turned back to her.

"We're going to trap the ghost," Rosenberg announced.

By her expression, Kay thought they were crazy. They held up their cameras.

"What you said earlier about witches gave me an idea," Rosenberg said. "You know how in some cultures, people think cameras can capture their spirits?"

"Yeah . . ." she answered, almost wincing with doubt.

Gyllenhal continued. "Well, this thing is pure spirit. And if it's true, maybe we can trap it in our cameras."

"That's just superstition. Like what I told you about the bodies in the peat bogs. They often are found with forked sticks holding down their limbs, and leather straps tied around their necks. This is to keep their spirits from roaming."

"See?" Rosenberg said.

Kay shook her head. "But it's superstition. That didn't *really* keep spirits from roaming. There were no spirits to roam."

"Well, what do you call the thing tearing up the castle?" Gyllenhal asked. "It may smell bad, but it's not just swamp gas."

Kay had to concede that point.

"And what if this stuff worked because people believed it worked?" offered Rosenberg. "Like the stake thing worked because the people of the time believed it. And the spirits didn't rise because when they were alive, they believed that if they had stakes on them, they couldn't."

Kay thought about that and laughed. "What do you Americans call that? Reaching?"

"It's worth a try," Rosenberg insisted. "If it stops this thing, then fine. If we get a cool picture of a ghost, we're famous."

"Win-win," Gyllenhal said.

"Okay," Kay told them, nodding slowly. "If your theory of the ghost believing in what could trap it is right, then you've got one big problem."

"What's that?" Gyllenhal looked at Rosenberg nervously.

"There were probably no cameras when this 'ghost,' or whatever it is, was alive. So it would not know what they were, let alone that it could trap them."

Rosenberg's and Gyllenhal's jaws dropped simultaneously.

"But maybe—" Rosenberg began hopefully. But it was a thin hope. And it was a hope he would never express verbally because he suddenly became aware of a strong rotting smell.

The ceiling above Kay began to drip boiling water and steaming algae. All three looked up at the same time as the blazing spirit descended rapidly, dropping into Kay.

Instantly her eyes went black.

"Shit!" Rosenberg gasped.

The possessed girl's skin smoked slightly, small boils rose, but not as rapidly as they had on the girl in the courtyard. Her mouth opened to allow her swelling black tongue to emerge. Water and steam guttered from her lips.

The pair turned away from the girl who was no longer Kay and ran. The corpse shambled after them. It could not control the body well enough to catch up.

As he had done outside, Rosenberg stopped short again.

"What the hell, Ben!" Gyllenhal said, stopping a few paces ahead and turning back. "You're gonna get us killed."

"We gotta try this," Rosenberg said, breathing heavily, frightened, yet resolute.

Gyllenhal admired his friend's conviction and raised his camera.

"You're right. Let's take one for the team!" he cried.

The Kay-thing rounded the corner, arms stretched before her, seemingly frustrated that the body could go no faster.

"Hit 'er!" Cameron yelled.

Flashes went off. Kay's bulging eyes blinked, and she paused her advance for a moment in confusion.

"Hey," Rosenberg said, clicking away, his camera spewing instant pictures onto the floor, "this might be working."

"Yeah," Gyllenhal answered grimly.

No. She began her advance again. Her claws reached for them and she began to cough slime. Was she laughing at their impending doom?

"Abort, Pete, abort!" Rosenberg yelled as he dropped his camera.

They turned together and ran.

This time, Gyllenhal stopped short and choked out a cry. Rosenberg watched as his friend shot backward. The creature had snagged his camera strap and was dragging him toward her. The creature's free hand clawed to find purchase on Gyllenhal's shoulder.

He turned instantly to help his friend.

"No frickin' way!" he yelled and reached up to his friend's neck where the camera was, pulled tight under his chin. He quickly slipped his hand between the camera and Gyllenhal's neck.

"Duck, Pete."

With Rosenberg providing tension in the other direction, Gyllenhal was able to duck free of the camera strap. Rosenberg let go of the camera suddenly, causing the sputtering creature to stumble back a few steps. However, the camera caught Gyllenhal in the forehead as it flew past him and he fell to the ground.

The creature nearly fell over, but regained its balance.

Rosenberg reached down and pulled a groggy Gyllenhal to his feet.

"Come on!"

Knowing it was their final chance to escape, they turned.

Too late. Two hot, clammy hands grabbed the back of their heads and twisted them each inward so that they were facing each other. Kay slammed them together, the cracking of their foreheads echoing down the ancient hallway.

21

"Sofia!"

Cameron yelled as he raced into the room.

"In here!" Her voice rang out from the bathroom.

"Wait here," he told Harry and entered the bathroom. At the doorway, he screeched to a halt.

His father stood hunched over the sink, this time wearing his burial suit, pulling down his lower lids to examine his eyes. His skin was puffy and purple. And fragile—the lid tore away from one of his eyes and the shrunken orb popped out, dangling from a withered stalk of muscles.

"Oops," Cameron Senior said absently.

"What's up, Cam?" Harry called from the doorway. "She's not here."

Cameron backed through the doorway as his father turned toward him. An amused smile played on the ghost's rotting lips as he tucked the eye back into his head.

"I love that part," the ghost said to Cameron. Then, in a perfect imitation of Sofia's voice, he said, "Take me, Cameron, take me now!"

Cameron raised a hand to his mouth, horrified. Harry appeared beside him, following Cameron's gaze.

"You okay? What's up?"

Cameron pointed to his father, who emerged from the bathroom. "It's my dad."

"Huh?" Harry looked at the doorway and saw nothing.

Cameron's dad smiled again and shook his head.

"He can't see me and I've got no time left, so listen up." He stopped and leaned against the door frame. The flesh and pus oozing from his suit left a dark smear against the wood.

"What's going on, Cam?" Harry was tugging at Cameron's shoulder for them to get going. Cameron pushed him away.

"Hold up a sec."

Harry backed off and watched his friend converse with empty air.

"So we're here to talk about vengeance," Mr. Dean said. "You're not very focused."

"What are you talking about?"

"I asked for vengeance, and you crib from Edgar Allan Poe? You were never good with books, Cam. You're a guy of action. This was not action." He snorted in derision. "What's the KISS rule, buddy?"

"Keep It Simple Stupid," Cameron recited dutifully. "Come on, Dad, I'm not a kid."

"Aren't you?" he asked. "Vengeance is *one thing*, swift and terrible and *final*. What do I get? Hardy Boys crap and namby-pamby 'I don't want my wittle girlfriend to know she killed her own daddy.' "

"Dad—"

"Shut up!" his father commanded.

"I hate to interrupt your wigout, Cam," Harry said suddenly, "But we gotta find the others."

"Will you give me a second?" Cameron snapped. "I'm talking to my father!"

Ignoring Harry, he turned back to the ghost.

"Harry's right, Dad. In case you didn't know, there's this other ghost running around the castle right now."

The ghost seemed unconcerned. "That would be Ophelia. Now, *she* knows what vengeance is all about. Killing, Cam, plain and simple. Eye for an eye and all that."

"Look, when we've gotten out of—"

Mr. Dean's ghost suddenly darted forward and loomed over Cameron. Though they did not touch, Cameron could feel his father's presence like an infection spreading in his blood.

"Listen to me. Remember the first time we met and I mentioned a curse? Ophelia's your curse, son. She's after your soul's Siamese twin. She's going to use Sofia to tear your soul in half. Now, dead guys like us are interested in only one thing, avenging our wrongful deaths. But we all need instruments: you're mine, and Sofia's will be hers. And frankly, as much as I loved you when I was alive, being dead means I don't really care like I used to. But I do care about my own vengeance. But if you show up on the other side without having sent Claudia's black soul ahead of you, there will be hell to pay."

He smiled once more. "And you can take that phrase literally."

Cameron Dean, Sr.'s ghost faded. It took Cameron a moment to recover from that smile, a smile he hoped never to witness again.

He turned to Harry, who paced hopelessly next to him.

"Okay, we better go." They shot from the room and headed toward Harry and Shayne's room. As they walked, Cameron explained gravely, "When we find everyone, I want you to take Sofia and my mom with you, understand?"

"What about—?"

"You don't want to know. At least not up front." They stopped in the hallway. "Do you believe me about my aunt Claudia, that she killed my dad?"

"Yes." He didn't hesitate.

"Then when this is all over, no matter what happens, you've got to back me up." He paused, then added, "Whether I'm there to defend myself or not."

"What are you going to do?" Harry asked.

"Let's just say my dad just taught me about the birds and bees and leave it at that, okay?"

Harry nodded and they headed down the hallway toward his room. When they got there, it was empty. Nothing seemed changed from when Harry had come down for the party. Shayne had not been there.

"We have to keep going," Cameron told him. They left and continued down the passageway toward his mother's room on the opposite side of the castle.

Just as they rounded the next corner, they heard a scream. At the end of the hallway, Molly Ramirez was running toward them, pursued by the shimmering vortex of Ophelia. The floor hissed and steamed behind her.

"Help me!" Molly cried.

The boys didn't know what to do. To their left was a stairway. Moving quickly, Cameron dashed forward and seized Molly by the arm.

"In there!" he yelled at Harry, indicating the stairwell. Practically yanking Molly off her feet, they nearly fell into the stairwell. He started to go down, but saw a pair of corpses on the landing below. Molly started to scream and pull away.

"Grab her other arm!" Harry did as he was told and they hauled the hysterical Molly upstairs.

As they did so, Ophelia burned through the wall next to the doorway and flew up the stairs toward them.

"We can't outrun her that way," Harry cried.

Cameron realized he was right, and suddenly had a thought.

"Take her," he yelled out and let go of Molly's arm. He spun and faced Ophelia, between the ghost and her retreating friends. Cameron braced himself for impact. If he was wrong, he was done for. And with his father waiting with hellish punishment.

Ophelia stopped suddenly. She regarded him much like she did before, in the courtyard, but this time there was more anger and frustration than amusement. Her glow was noticeably dimmer.

Cameron heard the door slam to the floor above. Ophelia looked up too. The smile returned to her face.

She zoomed straight up into the ceiling.

"Damn!" Cameron yelled and took the steps three at a time to get upstairs.

When he burst out the door to the upper floor, Ophelia was just descending into Molly's body. She was screaming as it happened; she hadn't stopped screaming since they had encountered her. She stopped now, in a choking gurgle, as her lungs filled with hot fluid.

She became a statue, jerking Harry to a halt. He tried to let go, but she gripped his arm like a vise. She was crushing him.

"Hey, Ophelia!" Cameron shouted and barreled toward her. Molly's head jerked to the side, momentarily distracting her. Cameron hit her like freight train and she went down. Leaping to his feet, he stomped on her forearm. Bones snapped beneath his shoe.

She let go and in the same moment, he pulled his friend from the ground by his good arm. They ran away down the corridor, Harry holding his injured arm close to him. As they rounded the corner, Cameron looked back.

Ophelia's spirit rose from Molly's body, then sank into the floor.

A third of the way down the long hallway, Cameron stopped Harry.

"Let's look at that arm real quick."

"Not here," Harry told him. "Not out in the open."

Cameron thought about it for a moment. "Well, everything's out in the open when the thing that can get you walks through walls."

But Harry looked afraid, as well as hurt.

"Okay, Harry," he said and tried the nearest door. It was locked. "This way," he said and they tried all the doors down the corridor in the direction of his mother's room. One finally opened and they ducked in.

The door struck something hard as Cameron opened it and he looked behind the door to see what it was. The curtains were drawn, leaving the room in gray shadow. Something round had rolled away from the door and rocked to a stop a few feet away. Cameron stooped to pick it up. His hands fell upon something slick and hairy. Grabbing it by a loose tuft, he picked it up and held it close in the dim light.

And nearly vomited.

"Oh, God! It's Eric!" Dangling before him was the severed head of his teammate and friend. "I knew him really well, Harry. Hell of a player, and funny guy."

Cameron suddenly felt dizzy. An image of him and Eric as children rose unbidden in his mind: Eric, a big kid even then, giving him a piggyback ride down the street because he had lost a bet that involved eating worms. It should have been embarrassing, but Eric had made quite the show of it. The ride ended with both of them rolling around Cameron's front lawn in childish hysterics.

"Geez, Eric," Cameron said aloud. "This is *so* not funny."

"I thought I knew him, Cam," Harry said gravely, bringing him back to the present. "And her too."

Cameron turned to see that Harry was not looking at Eric's head. Instead, he was looking at a dark lump in the bed. They approached, but Cameron knew what lay there before he even got a good look.

Shayne. Dead. Drowned.

And she had been cheating on Harry with Eric.

Harry suddenly collapsed to his knees, weeping against his good arm. Cameron gingerly set Eric's head down, pushing it out of sight with his foot as he went to console his friend.

"I'm sorry, Harry. I don't know what to say."

Harry continued to sob.

Cameron let him continue for a few moments, then squeezed his shoulder.

"We gotta get going, Harry. This isn't over yet."

Seconds later, Harry collected himself. He stood stiffly, turned and walked out of the room into the hallway. He didn't look back.

22

The anniversary clock ticked its way loudly toward midnight, just under an hour away. The scraping of flats on stone provided a counterpoint to the ticking as Claudia paced back and forth before the clock.

"He'd better get here soon," she said in agitation. "Or I'm going to have to send someone out to bring him here."

The scream of another dying boy rose from somewhere outside the door. This one ended abruptly.

The castle had filled with bloodcurdling screams like a neighborhood haunted house at Halloween. Except, these sounded real and varied, not canned and repetitive. Once they had begun, Claudia only paid attention to make sure the voice crying out was not Cameron's. His death by anyone else's hands but her own would ruin everything.

Whoever was rampaging through the castle right now better not spoil her plans. Sofia had insisted a ghost was after her. But then, the girl was barely coherent when Claudia sneaked up on her and had smashed Sofia's face into the bathroom mirror.

She looked down at the bed, upon which the girl lay bound beside Geri, who was similarly bound. Both women were gagged. Sofia sported a nasty cut on her forehead. The pillow beneath her head was smeared with blood and sweat.

Thanks to the mayhem in the castle around them, Claudia had been able to push and drag the semiconscious girl through the hallways unchallenged. Still, the going was slow and if Claudia hadn't encountered her "assistant" along the way, she might have disposed of Sofia before she got the girl back to her room. After all, in the long run, Sofia didn't really need to be alive. Cameron would come to their room just to find his mother. But killing Cameron in front of both of them would be much more satisfying.

As she tied Sofia in strips sheared from the bed linens, the girl muttered almost constantly about someone named Ophelia, for whom she often mistook herself. When she was more self-aware, she identified Ophelia as a ghost who was seeking revenge for some ancient wrong.

Ghost, huh? Claudia thought. *Fuck with me and I'll find a way to bring you back to life just to torture you to death.*

Her initial terror upon listening to the party band's song had given way to a brilliant clarity. Cameron had been taunting her all along and the song was his final challenge. He wanted a showdown, and she meant to give it to him.

No more of this underhanded, indirect poisoning crap. She was going to carpe his diem and his dinero, stare him in the eye as she killed him in front of his fiancée and mother. And best of all, she intended to be filing her nails the whole time. In the morning, she would tell her story, alternating between sobs and an eerie calm for effect, of how she barely survived the tragedy at Castle Elsinore.

Her nephew, still grieving over his dead father and unable to cope with his new fortune, went crazy and killed his fiancée. She herself is about to be killed, but is saved at the last second by . . . and at this point in her story she would lay her head in her hands and sob, for her savior had died as well.

The rampage downstairs would only help. If the real culprit escaped, then the deaths could be blamed on Cameron. The strategically planted cyanide would show that Cameron's plans included mass murder. Claudia would receive this news with appropriate confusion and horror.

After delivering her heartrending, horrifying story, she would leave this country, a mute, emotionally blasted Geri at her side. Claudia would be a free woman, and soon after her return to the States, a very *rich* woman.

* * *

The screams of the dying were becoming more infrequent. The ghost was running out of victims; they had either fled or she had killed them already. That meant Cameron and Harry, and presumably Sofia and his mother, were on the short list. Cameron hoped Aunt Claudia had already been checked off, but knew he couldn't get that lucky. His father had made it quite clear that Claudia's death was his responsibility. And so he would finally accept that responsibility, and take her life.

"Hey, isn't that that Danish girl Eric came with?" Harry pointed to a body in the hallway ahead of them. Scattered around the corpse were black rectangles framed in white: Polaroids, they discovered upon further inspection. Cameron ignored the photos, except to note that they and the object lying near her head did not bode well for more friends of theirs.

He picked up the multicolored strap with a camera dangling from it. The lens was smashed.

"This is Gyllenhal's camera."

A large splatter of blood stained the stone floor a few feet ahead of the body. Not far from that, a rag.

Approaching the rag, they saw it was a shirt. Cameron recognized it as Rosenberg's. It was drenched in blood. More clothes lay beyond this one, all with telltale dark stains.

"I don't like the look of this," Harry told him as they followed the clothes, which lay like a trail down the hall. Each one they inspected was bloody and torn.

"It looks like they've been torn apart!" Cameron nodded grimly. He had seen Eric's head, so he knew it was entirely possible.

The cuff of a pair of khakis stuck out from the bottom of a door several feet away. They had bunched up, preventing the door from closing completely.

Harry pushed open the door. It swung open with a creak and the meager light from the hallway dimly illuminated the room.

A dark lump lay sprawled on the bed. Irregular darker patches covered it. They soon recognized the skinny shape of Gyllenhal, naked, and covered in blood. The black clump on his face was his broken nose. As they approached, another dark area of the bed resolved itself into an arm. Cameron walked around the foot of the bed to find Rosenberg, seemingly half-crouched, his arm still draped on the bed. He too was covered in blood.

Neither were moving.

Cameron stood and sadly pronounced what seemed obvious to him and Harry both: "Rosenberg and Gyllenhal are dead."

The lights that once festooned the castle for Ophelia's dead eyes had gone dark. Only a few remained. A crucial few.

Through her killings, she had dissipated much of the energy she had collected from the stage electronics. She was harmless to males in her spirit form once more, and the females died with lungs filled with swamp water. Their brains no longer boiled in their skulls, eyes shooting out like broken steam valves.

Sofia would now not die too quickly when she took her. But Ophelia was plenty powerful enough to take the girl.

She had sought out every flame of love, whether it burned bright as a torch or flickered like a firefly, and snuffed it. As her love had been snuffed.

And then the greatest vengeance of all was yet to come. She would douse the brightest flame of all, the love between Sofia and Cameron, and then be reunited in eternity with her own love, Hamlet.

Their love would end. Hers would begin and last until the end of time.

She laughed and raised her fists in anticipation of her coming triumph.

But she didn't feel triumphant. Not quite.

I didn't do anything, she suddenly pouted to herself. Then pointedly, she corrected her thoughts. *Sofia* had done nothing. The flip-flops of identity had continued to plague her, but now she was used to them. She even sympathized.

At least the others she had killed would likely end up together in eternity. Sofia would be used to kill her love, and be doomed to wander the afterlife alone.

It's not fair, Ophelia thought with Sofia's mind.

Tell it to the swamp, she replied to the voice in her head. Bring your case to the algae and the worms, the dead leaves and the leeches. Cry out to the bog. See what they think is fair.

But it's not, said the Sofia part of her in a tiny voice. And then she was silent.

She sensed movement. Above, Cameron made his way toward Sofia. Excellent. Below, a pair of stragglers, who had been hiding in the library, decided to emerge because the castle had fallen silent.

Their screams filled the air of the castle moments later. Their heads would be found mounted on the walls among the guns and hunting trophies.

"Huh?" came a groggy, surprised voice.

At the door, Cameron and Harry, turned back in shock. Gyllenhal was pulling himself up to a sitting position on the bed.

"Oh, my nose," he said in a deeply nasal voice, prodding his broken nose gingerly. He spied Rosenberg's arm on the bed and poked it. "Hey bunghole, wake up!"

"Huh?" Rosenberg's equally nasal voice rose from behind the bed. Suddenly, he was laughing. "Wow, Pete, You were ama—" He stopped himself as his head rose above the mattress and he spied Cameron and Harry watching them wide-eyed. "Um."

He ducked down behind the bed, scrambling to find clothes that weren't there. "It's not what you think, guys," he said quickly.

Gyllenhal shook his head and turned to the pair in the doorway. "Fuck it. Sure it is."

At that, Rosenberg's head shot up above the mattress again. He was about to protest, but suddenly changed his mind.

"We're probably gonna die here anyway, so what the hell?" he said. Then, "Could you throw us our clothes?"

Cameron laughed, and Harry dashed out to gather up their clothes with his good arm.

Moments later, as they dressed, the pair explained their conversation with Kay and her subsequent possession. Though the cameras hadn't captured the ghost, it had slowed her down. She collapsed just after slamming their faces together, breaking their noses. Intensely relieved at narrowly escaping death, they hugged, oblivious of the blood pouring out of their nostrils and onto each other.

"And yadda yadda yadda, you found us," Gyllenhal finished quickly.

Rosenberg looked up sheepishly as he buttoned his shirt.

"Listen, Ben," Cameron told him. "You tell me what's weirder, that you two finally realized what everyone's known all along, or that a ghost is going around murdering people. You tell me what I should be more freaked out by."

He had meant to reassure Rosenberg, but the younger boy was frowning.

"I'm serious," Cameron insisted.

"No, I just thought of something," Rosenberg said and darted out the door. "Bring the newspaper, Pete," he yelled. Gyllenhal grabbed something from their dresser and followed Rosenberg into the hall, Cameron and Harry close behind.

They found Rosenberg crouched over Kay's body. At first, they thought he was searching the body. Instead he was collecting the Polaroids scattered around it.

"Look at this," he said, standing suddenly. Cameron took the photos and looked at them. He whistled at what they showed and passed them on. Gyllenhal whooped when he saw them.

The photos showed Kay charging forward. It looked like a scene out of a zombie movie. But the pictures showed more than just Kay. Around her was what at first appeared to be a colorful smear. Staring at it, the smear resolved itself into a shape, the shape of a person, as if superimposed on Kay.

It was the ghost.

"We did it!" Gyllenhal shouted. "We've got a real ghost on film! We'll be rich!"

"That's not what I mean," Rosenberg said, oddly serious. "Look at her face."

Cameron and Harry got behind Gyllenhal and they studied the ghostly smear. Squinting, details of the ghost resolved themselves. It was like looking into a Magic Eye poster. Her face became quite clear.

"Pretty," Gyllenhal said.

"Now, check out the picture in the newspaper," Rosenberg told them.

Gyllenhal lifted the paper and opened it to the page of the nearby excavation.

"Holy crap!" Gyllenhal whistled. "It's her."

Though the face of the ancient woman in the inset was a deep brown, her eyes closed and expressionless, the resemblance between her and the ghost was unmistakable.

"See, Pete? No forked sticks." Rosenberg tapped a finger to the full shot, and Gyllenhal nodded slowly.

"So what?" asked Cameron. He was intrigued, but didn't see the point.

"We can stop her," Rosenberg told them.

He recounted the legend Kay had told them, of the days when the bodies of witches were cast out into peat bogs, and that to keep their souls from roaming, the superstitious would stake their limbs to the ground.

"We can go there and stake her limbs. That'll pin her soul in one place. She can't hurt us anymore."

Cameron and Harry could only stare at him.

"Look, we couldn't trap her soul by taking pictures, okay?" Gyllenhal told them. "Maybe Kay was right, that we couldn't because in the ghost's life, they never had cameras and so didn't have that sort of belief. But the custom of staking bodies to keep souls from roaming probably dates back to before the ghost's time. So it's worth a shot."

Cameron was still staring in disbelief, but not at the absurdity of Gyllenhal's argument. His fearless conviction amazed Cameron. He no longer saw hero-worship or even the need for approval in either of their eyes. They were simply presenting their beliefs, with no desperate need for affirmation. Rosenberg and Gyllenhal had grown up.

He wondered briefly whether his own transition from virginity had been that stark and effective.

"At this point, nothing can hurt. And if nothing else, you guys will get away from this place."

Rosenberg reached out and grasped his shoulder tightly. "That's not why we're going, Cam. We're not abandoning you."

Cameron smiled back and squeezed his arm in return. "I know that. Go for it, guys."

The quartet split up: Rosenberg and Gyllenhal to the peat bog, Cameron and Harry to Geri and Claudia's room.

Harry fell silent for a few minutes, rubbing his injured arm. The doors and columns on either side of them seemed to pass in an infinite, repeating pattern. The hallway seemed to stretch on forever. They heard one more muffled shout, paused momentarily, then continued when they were sure that it wasn't Rosenberg or Gyllenhal.

"So what're you going to do, Cam?" Harry finally asked.

"Well, falling out of towers is popular this time of year," he said. Neither of them laughed. "You know I have to do this."

Harry nodded.

Around them, the place grew silent as a crypt. Midnight was near and twilight hung around them, absorbing all sounds. If anyone else remained in the castle, living, dead or dying, Cameron couldn't tell. Nor did he cast his thoughts anywhere but up ahead.

The door that seemed so interminably far away suddenly loomed up as if it were trying to meet him halfway. And just like that, he and Harry stood before it.

Cameron put his hand on the doorknob and Harry stood behind him ready to follow.

"No," Cameron told him. "Stay out here and watch out. And I mean that in about a zillion ways." They shared a tired smile. The strange peace that had settled upon the place was allowing their exhaustion to catch up with them.

"You need to be able to tell people what happened, but you don't have to watch it happen," Cameron said.

Harry agreed to stay put. So Cameron faced the door, took a deep breath and turned the handle.

23

The last of the castle's white gravel crunched underfoot as Rosenberg and Gyllenhal passed through the enormous wrought-iron gates. Beyond, a paved road wound down the hill, trees grown close on either side like a modern highway through a Grimm's fairy tale wood. After their experiences in Castle Elsinore, the pair would have been relieved to meet up with a hungry wolf or ogre.

The density of the branches above blocked out the low sun, making it suddenly as dark as it would normally be so close to midnight. They kept a slow, steady pace until their eyes adjusted to the gloom, then took off in a trot down the road.

After a few minutes the woods began to thin once more, the landscape brightening. Soon, they emerged into the valley below the castle. Immediately, a rich, smoky and not-unpleasant odor greeted them.

Farmhouses could be seen scattered in the couple of miles between the forest and town, where the road led after a few gentle turns. Dim figures could be seen scurrying back and forth in the well-lit main street of Kronborg. The Elsinore survivors had reached the town.

"I hope they sort themselves out soon," Rosenberg commented. "Even if this works, they're going to need help up there."

"Yup," Gyllenhal replied, half-listening, half-searching the horizon to get their bearings. Soon, he pointed. "Over there."

A low, makeshift hut could be seen in a distant field. They veered off the road and stepped into soft, spongy turf.

"Ugh," Gyllenhal said, stopping momentarily, lifting his feet, one by one, to keep from sinking into the ground. It was like mud, but firmer.

"Peat," Rosenberg said.

"What?"

"No, not you," Rosenberg snapped. He pointed to the ground. "P-e-a-t. We're in a peat bog. That's what the smell is."

"Ah," Gyllenhal answered and they continued, squishing their way across the bog.

"Whoa! Wait!" Rosenberg said suddenly. They stopped. "Nearly forgot," he told Gyllenhal. "Wait here."

Turning, he ran back toward the road and into the forest. Gyllenhal returned to stepping from foot to foot lightly, trying not to let the marshy ground seep into his shoes. From inside the forest, wood snapped sharply and soon, Rosenberg trotted back out from the darkness.

He held up four Y-shaped branches.

"Forgot to bring the handcuffs," he said brightly.

Gyllenhal smiled. "Good idea," he smirked.

"Shut up!" Rosenberg said shortly, embarrassed, but smiling despite himself. "I meant for the body."

Gyllenhal said nothing, and they both ran toward the shack in the distance, secret smiles playing on both of their faces, each of their minds bouncing from one unorthodox thought to another.

Cameron stepped through the door to his mother's room without knocking. His heart stopped at the sight of Sofia and his mother bound and gagged, lying side by side on the bed.

"Sofia! Mom!" he cried, kickstarting his heart, which now raced as he flew to their side. Using both hands, he tore the gags away from their faces. "Are you hurt?" he asked quickly.

"No, but—" his mother said weakly.

"Honey, what's wrong?" Sofia looked bleary-eyed and feverish. He turned to his mother, who was holding up her hands to be untied. "What's wrong with Sofia?" he asked as he tugged the bonds loose.

Before his mother could answer, a voice behind him spoke.

"She thinks she's some medieval girl, apparently."

Cameron turned to find Claudia sitting on a chair near the balcony doors. She sat cross-legged and sidesaddle, filing her nails as if she hadn't a care in the world. She wasn't even looking up.

Cameron took a trembling step forward.

"Did you do this?" he asked. His fists were clenched at his side.

Claudia looked up languidly. "Yes, sorry Cam. Your girlfriend—oh, excuse me, fiancée—was a little agitated. As for your mother,"—she raised an eyebrow and sneered—"she's used to it."

"You bitch!" He took another step forward.

She abruptly swiveled forward in the chair, causing Cameron to halt. Then she relaxed again and resumed filing her nails.

"I've been called worse," she shrugged.

"Like 'Claud.'" Cameron drenched the word in contempt. His aunt paused momentarily, stopped filing her nails and stood.

"Sticks and stones, you little shit," she sneered. "Your father was shit, too. And look where that got him. Well, guess where it's gonna get *you*."

He unclenched his fists and beckoned her forward.

"Think you can take me, old woman?" he challenged. "Come on, then."

Claudia just laughed.

"How very *West Side Story*," she said, and sat back down. She resumed filing her nails, and resembled an insolent cat. "I don't rumble. Besides, I'm not really who you have to worry about."

Cameron was instantly on the alert, his eyes searching the room.

"Larry!" Claudia cried out.

With that, a balcony door swung open from the outside. Sofia's brother shambled through the doorway.

"Hey, Cam," Larry said in a voice more nasal and monotone than ever. His backpack was slung over his shoulder. But instead of his usual wavering gaze, he stared directly at Cameron.

"Hey—" Cameron could tell that Larry was off, somehow.

"So, like, you killed my dad," he said, no emotion in his voice. His eyes told another story, however.

"No—" Cameron began. "What're you talking about?"

Larry started to sway side to side.

"I found him like that, Cameron," Claudia announced. "Rocking back and forth, mumbling to himself. He helped me bring his sister here, you know."

"Larry," Cameron said and took a step forward. Larry quickly stepped back, his eyes suddenly alert. Cameron stayed put. "I don't know what she told you, but it's a lie. She's the murderer. She killed my dad. She probably killed yours!"

Larry looked from Cameron to Claudia, the slightest amount of confusion flickering in his eyes.

"Did you see him, Larry?" Cameron asked. "Did you see your dad somewhere?"

"No," Larry answered. More doubt. *Good,* Cameron thought.

Claudia simply laughed as she gently pushed back her cuticles with an orangewood stick she produced from her pocket.

"Show him what you did find, Larry," she said.

Without looking, Larry reached back and plucked something from his backpack. He held it up: frozen golden goose droppings.

"I gave this to Dad for Father's Day, did you know that?" Larry said, still holding the tie clip out. "It was the only time he ever thanked me. And he always wore it. Because of this, I knew that one day, he'd treat me the way he's always treated Sofia." He glanced at his sister without malice. But when his gaze returned to Cameron, dark fury burned from his eyes.

"Then you gave him that stupid other tie clip. It's like you wanted to take that away from me." He started rocking again. "You wanted to take him away from me. And then he was gone. I thought we were friends, Cameron. Why would you take my father away from me? Isn't my sister enough for you?"

"Larry, calm down." But Larry kept rocking.

"Tell him where you found it," Claudia said. "And what else you found." She then turned to Cameron. "All this plotting and planning to steal your inheritance, and it turns out you did my work for me. I just wish I would have known sooner. Now it's too late. For all of us."

Larry jabbed the tie clasp toward Cameron. "I found this in your room. It was on the floor, under the vanity table."

"Bastard got in there before me!" Claudia said. "If I had seen it, you wouldn't have lived even to now."

"I couldn't find anything else, not in the room," Larry continued. "Then I went outside. I saw the bushes, Cam. Did you push my dad out the window? Because he didn't want you to marry Sofia?" The swaying became more violent. Tears oozed from his eyes. "Did you kill my dad, Cameron?"

Cameron was about to accuse Claudia again, and then realized there was no point. Larry was devastated. *Poor guy,* he thought. He could no longer pretend he didn't know the truth. But that didn't mean he had to tell the entire truth, either. He glanced at Sofia and his mother. Sofia remained tied and mostly oblivious to the proceedings. Geri hadn't moved, other than to clutch her freed hands to her chest and wring them.

"It was an accident, Larry," he said matter-of-factly. And that's as close to the facts as he would go. "We argued about the engagement. It got rough . . . and then . . . well . . ."

Once the words were spoken, Larry became placid again. He put the tie clip into his pocket and regarded Cameron thoughtfully. His manic rocking had ceased.

"Tell you what. How about one more game of Rock, Paper, Scissors? If you win, then I'll forgive you. If I win, then you gotta pay me what I owe you. I think it'll be," he looked up and thought for a moment, "uh, forty million dollars. You could afford that, I think, to live happily ever after with my sister, huh?"

"You don't have to—" Cameron began, but Larry cut him off.

"No, *you* have to." This time, Larry's voice was fierce, his eyes blazing. Cameron saw that he had no choice.

Claudia had stopped filing her nails again and was looking up with interest.

Cameron knew this had to be a trick, since Larry had never won a game of Rock, Paper, Scissors in his life. So there was a catch. But Cameron felt he had to play it through. "I'll be okay."

"I'll count," Larry said, his voice back to a drone. He stepped forward and the two faced each other. "Hand behind your back," Larry said next. Cameron stared at the dull boy in front of him. He couldn't fathom what would come next.

"Rock . . ." Larry started slowly, "Paper . . . Scissors!"

Cameron thrust his hand forward, his fingers splayed. Paper.

Larry, however, pinwheeled his arm over his head and with blinding speed struck Cameron on the side of the face. His hand held a large rock he had pulled from his backpack.

Geri screamed.

Cameron was knocked back by the blow and fell to the floor. Trying to remain conscious, he looked up with vision blurred by blood running into his swelling eye.

Above him, Larry stood, his face on fire with rage and grief. Blood and flesh dripped from the rock in his hand.

"Rock beats paper," Larry roared. "Rock beats you!" And he raised his hand to strike another blow.

They were together now. And they were the only ones left. Ophelia could see their lights, those of Cameron and Sofia, blazing above. They were surrounded by several, far dimmer lights and one that appeared to her like a dancing black flame, the only other living beings in the castle. The others were of little importance. Now, vengeance would be hers.

She blazed straight up through two floors of the castle and arrived at the end of a long hallway. At the other end were her prey, and her destiny.

She was their destiny, and Hamlet's eternity. Savoring the anticipation, she glided, slowly at first, then with increasing speed, toward the doorway between her and her vengeance.

* * *

Harry listened at the door, hearing muffled voices and some shouting. But the wood and stone robbed the sounds of any clarity. There was a scream, perhaps the sound of a scuffle, and Harry put a hand on the door handle, about to burst in and help his friend, injured arm or not. Then he stopped. Cameron had made it clear that Harry must not intrude.

Still, he was filled with nervous energy and paced before the door like a lion in a cage. There had been no sounds from elsewhere in the castle for quite some time. Perhaps the ghost had left, giving chase to those who had fled.

The shimmer that suddenly appeared at the opposite end of the hallway disabused him of that notion.

It hovered for a moment, as if gathering its strength. Then it bobbed forward, gliding at first at a steady pace. As it neared, however, its speed picked up. Steam rose in its wake; slime dripped from the ceiling. Light fixtures sizzled and burst as it neared.

The ghost flew swiftly now. It wasn't nearly as distinct as it had been after it had fried the band, but the general shape was unmistakable—a small woman with flowing hair. It barreled toward him.

He knocked on the door, but did not open it.

"Cam? Cam? Something . . . *it*, is coming. *Cam!*"

There was no reply from inside. When he turned

back toward the hallway, the thing was almost upon him. It shot like a fiery cannonball at him.

Harry dived aside just in time. As he struck the floor, the ghost passed into the room, leaving its steaming, fetid mark on the door.

24

The hut was unguarded and unlit. It was crudely fashioned with aluminum poles over which a ragged canvas tarp was drawn to protect the site from the elements. The canvas flap hung motionless, and the dim light gave everything a flat, grainy illumination.

"I guess this isn't a high crime area," Rosenberg commented at the openness of the excavation. Gyllenhal glanced back toward the castle.

"Not until tonight, I bet," he said gravely.

Beneath the center of the tarp was an oblong opening, about three feet by six feet, looking very much like an open grave. They knew instinctively that it was. Closer inspection revealed a strange difference. This grave had not been dug. The peat and mud edging the opening appeared rounded and grooved, as if the mud had boiled away from the opening, ran off like water then suddenly refroze.

This gibed with what they had seen of the ghost.

"This is our girl," Gyllenhal said. Rosenberg nodded in agreement.

"But where is she?"

She was close. About ten feet beyond the main shack was a second, smaller tent they had not seen upon their approach. Within it lay something covered in a white tarp. Preparing themselves—at this point they both knew it was conceivable that the body would suddenly reanimate at their touch—they gave each other a silent "ready-set-go" count and pulled away the tarp.

Ophelia looked little changed from the photograph in the newspaper. Now, however, she was real and not a collection of ink dots on low-grade paper. And she smelled pretty bad. Otherwise, she looked like a lifelike oiled-leather doll, brown and moist-skinned, curled on her side as if asleep. Rosenberg looked closer. A wreath of flowers had been preserved around her head. She even still had fingerprints.

"She'll last a little while longer like this," he said, trying to breathe through his mouth, "but not for long, even in this temperature. Too much oxygen." He handed his friend two of the sticks.

"Wait," Gyllenhal said. "Shouldn't we put her back, in her original resting place?"

Rosenberg considered for a moment, then nodded. "Yeah, if this is gonna work at all, it'll work best if she's back on, or in, familiar ground."

Rosenberg went down to her feet, Gyllenhal stayed by her shoulders. Grimacing, they reached down and wedged their hands beneath her body.

She was wet and slick to the touch, like a dense sponge soaked in motor-oil.

"One, two, *three!*" Rosenberg counted out and they heaved Ophelia's body up. For a small body, it weighed a great deal. Secretly both were worried about a limb tearing loose, sending the body splattering to the ground and leaving one or both of them holding a severed limb.

They got the body back to its original grave without incident, however, and gently lowered it into the hole. Once it was settled, Rosenberg retrieved the branches they had left under the smaller tent and returned to the grave. There was just enough room on either side of the body for them to jump down into it.

"Here goes nuthin'," he said to Gyllenhal as he handed him two of the branches.

Just then, a shot rang out in the distance.

After the third savage blow he dealt to Cameron, Larry threw the rock aside. The football hero lay at his feet, his head pouring blood, but still conscious and writhing in pain.

Just how he wanted him.

Cameron's mom continued to scream as she struggled with the binds around her ankles. Sofia remained semiconscious next to her on the bed.

For her part, Claudia sat placidly in her chair, as if watching a particularly well-staged opera from box seats.

Larry unslung his bag from his shoulder and reached into it.

"Paper wins, too!" he cried and pulled out a sheaf of invitations to the banquet, their first night in the castle. He took a handful and crumpled them into a ball.

"Larry—" Cameron choked out. He reached a hand out weakly. Larry knocked it aside and started jamming wads of paper into Cameron's mouth. He tried to scoot away, but Larry dropped onto his chest, knocking the breath out of him and pinning him down. The crazed boy continued to shove paper down Cameron's throat. He was choking.

But not too quickly, Larry thought with relish.

He stood and reached into his backpack for his final item.

"Scissors ends the game!" Larry said, holding up the gardening shears from the shed. Straddling Cameron once more, he raised the shears above his head, handles up, blades down. The muscles in his arms tensed as he prepared to end Cameron's life.

There was a knock at the door. Harry's muffled voice called through:

"Cam? Cam? Something . . . *it,* is coming. *Cam!*"

Larry paused to look at the door, but Claudia snapped at him from her chair.

"Ignore him. Finish it. Avenge your father's murder."

But before he could, the door exploded. It didn't shatter—the door remained intact and closed—but something burst through it, a thing of light and water and foul odor.

The ghost.

Larry nearly fell backward out of surprise and watched the glowing apparition circle the room twice, then plunge toward the bed. It seemed to disappear into Sofia. She immediately started choking and steam rose from her mouth.

While Larry was stunned, Geri leapt shrieking at him from the bed. She struck at his shoulder, knocking him away from Cameron. He dropped the shears beside Cameron and landed on his back at Claudia's feet.

"You stay away from my son!" Geri screamed. Grabbing the shears, she rose awkwardly to her feet.

Through Cameron's blood-pink view of the world, he could see his mother standing above him, brandishing the large blades.

No one in the room was more shocked than Claudia, who stood quickly.

"What's this, Geri? Put those down, right away, before you hurt yourself!"

"What, so you and that maniac can kill my son? I don't think so, *Claudia.*"

Larry had scrambled to his feet and walked toward her with raised hands. He suddenly adopted a little-boy voice.

"I'm sorry, Mrs. Dean. Just give them to me, I won't do it again."

Geri replied by spitting at him. She jabbed the shears in his direction and he had to dodge the blades.

"To hell with both of you!" she cried and took a step forward.

She had never managed to untie the bindings on her ankles and in her fury, had forgotten. Her feet caught and she toppled over. She threw her hands out to brace herself for the fall, but she was also still holding the shears. Larry had no time to dodge and the blades plunged into his chest, piercing both of his lungs. He fell backward, choking, into Claudia, who was knocked backward into her chair.

Larry turned to her, crying tearlessly, spat a mouthful of blood into her face and died.

Claudia screamed in terror and rage, pushed the boy's corpse off of her and stood. She hauled Geri to her feet by the neck of her nightgown.

"Fine time for a show of guts, Geri," she growled. "Now we've *all* got blood on our hands."

"I've had blood on my hands ever since I let you kill my husband," Geri answered back.

Claudia appeared to boil over then, and raised a hand to strike. But Geri did not look away or wince.

She continued to look into Claudia's eyes steadily. Claudia softened and lowered her hands.

"I did love you, you know," she said softly. She reached for Geri's face and drew her in. At first, Geri resisted, then gave in, allowing herself to be kissed by the woman who had attempted to kill her son. She had allowed herself to be kissed this way after the same woman had killed her husband. Claudia's hands had caressed her face so gently then. It felt that way again.

Suddenly, the grip on her face tightened and Claudia twisted her head abruptly to the left, breaking her neck. The smallest amount of regret Claudia felt for any of her terrible acts died with Geri.

"I loved you," she continued in a dull voice. "I don't remember when anymore."

And she let Geri drop to the floor.

"Okay, I'd say we've got about a minute or so before we're riddled with bullets," Rosenberg said.

The gunshot had come from the farm in the distance. Apparently, they had been discovered after all.

"We wouldn't be riddled," Gyllenhal told him. "Shotguns don't fire that fast. Unless you're talking about the buckshot."

"Well, it would suck to go either way, considering the more esoteric opportunities to die that we've had tonight."

"True. Let's do this."

In the distance, they could see figures trudging through the bog in their direction. One pointed a shotgun at the sky and fired again.

"Why don't you come with me," Claudia roared and hauled Cameron to his feet. She shoved him toward the balcony. He slammed against the glass door, making it rattle. As he struggled to regain his balance and his wits, Claudia wiped the blood from her face.

"I hate a mess," she told him. "That's why I poisoned your father. I have to say this is much more satisfying, despite the messiness."

As she approached, Cameron swung out a fist. Claudia dodged it easily and its drunken momentum took it through a pane of glass in the other door. Glass tinkled to the ground. Cameron drew his hand back, tearing a deep gash on the jagged remains of the window.

"Ah, the great Cameron Dean, never one to give up without a fight," she taunted. "Usually not one to lose at all, I seem to remember. Well, welcome to your first and last crushing defeat."

Cameron lashed out again, but he didn't come close.

Suddenly, a snapping sound drew Claudia's attention. She turned toward it and found Sofia sitting up in bed. Another snapping sound followed—Sofia breaking her restraints simply by flexing her hands.

"Come to join the fun, dear?" Claudia asked. The

girl looked wild, her eyes black, her lips even blacker. The way Claudia saw it, the girl would soon be lying at the base of the tower, probably looking a lot worse.

Sofia began to slowly climb from the bed.

"It'll be quicker if you come to me. I'm getting a little tired hauling people all over this castle."

At that moment Cameron tackled Claudia and knocked her to the ground. She collapsed with a grunt.

Fighting to maintain consciousness, trying to keep the pain in his head from swallowing him whole, Cameron scrambled up Claudia's body to pin her arms.

He was too slow. She withdrew her nail file from her pocket and plunged it into his neck.

"Self-defense," she gasped as Cameron rolled away, clutching at his neck. "I won't even be lying when I have to tell that one." She was trying to maintain her bravado, but the strain of the ordeal was catching up with her.

At the side of the bed, Sofia stood immobile.

"How kind of you to wait your turn," Claudia snarled at her as she climbed onto Cameron's chest. His hand was still scratching at his neck, trying to grab hold of the file embedded there. Slick with blood, his fingers kept slipping from it. Claudia easily pulled his hand away and tucked it under her legs. She had pinned him as he had intended to pin her.

"Looking for this?" Claudia asked, grasping the bloody file. Getting a good grip on it, she twisted it inside the wound.

Cameron gargled a scream. The pain nearly made him black out for good that time. Only the sight of Sofia standing near the bed gave him a reason to stay conscious.

But why wasn't she helping him?

25

Ophelia entered the room and circled it once. Cameron was battling another youth. Though obviously more powerful than his opponent, he was losing. Then she saw the woman in the bed, the one next to her vessel.

Sofia! She insisted to herself. *I'm no one's vessel!* The moment's disorientation caused her to circle again. Meanwhile, the boy prepared to bring the blades down on Cameron, which would sever her from Hamlet forever.

Luckily, the fallen boy's mother interceded in time.

With that, she dropped into Sofia's body.

Her preternatural senses gave way to physical sensations, like the coppery smell of blood pervading the room, the sounds of screaming and a struggle, and the inevitable drowning sensation. But Ophelia had grown in power and experience. She had practiced with the other bodies. Sofia's death would be prolonged, not indefinitely, but with time enough for her to claim her eternal prize.

But Ophelia was alarmed at a new sensation: a tightness around her wrists and ankles.

The girl had been bound. Her attention had been distracted by the battle in the room, so she hadn't noticed.

No matter, Ophelia thought, and she began to strain at the ropes that bound her. Her strength would more than handle them.

"I've had about enough of this shit," Sofia said suddenly. From inside her own head. Ophelia tried to ignore the voice, which was quite different from her own disoriented thoughts, and tried to strain again at the bonds. She found the body unresponsive.

"You possess me, make me try to kill my boyfriend, end up killing my dad, then take most of my mind with you, make me channel all the girls you've killed, and now you're back for *more?* I think not."

The voice was echoing in her head. Mustering all her outrage and indignation, Ophelia roared back.

"Silence!" And for a moment, there *was* silence. It lasted long enough for her to pull apart her bonds like they were spider webs. She sat up in bed. With her mingled senses she could see that life had fled both Cameron's mother and the boy who had been threatening him. But now, the other woman, whose soul appeared as black fire, was stalking Cameron.

The woman paused momentarily, noticing that Ophelia/Sofia had risen. Then she was speaking, as if to Sofia herself. As she stood, Cameron knocked the woman to the floor.

This was her chance. She would take Cameron and together they would leap from the balcony and be held aloft by the winds of their destiny.

"Good Lord! Haven't you got enough modern girls in here to think of something a little less poofy? Geez!"

"Silence!" Ophelia cried again, but this time, Sofia resisted.

"Oh, silence yourself," she shot back. Sofia forced her head to tilt toward the battle raging before them. Claudia had turned the tables and had stabbed Cameron in the neck with a metal object. Sofia's voice became more frantic. "Look, she's killing him. But I'm not saving him just so we can go and kill him again. No way."

"You cannot stand in the way of my vengeance, my destiny."

"Do you see us doing anything *but* standing, swamp girl?"

And Ophelia noticed they were indeed not moving. Below them, the woman began to twist the metal instrument deeper into Cameron's neck. Blood gushed like a fountain. He would be dead soon, and she would be denied.

"Listen," Sofia said quickly, "what are you here for anyway, huh? What's this 'vengeance' you're talking about? Hey, I know times were different, but bad advice, especially from relatives, is bad advice, and there's no need to go crazy over it. And this Hamlet guy. If yours was such an inevitable, eternal love, then why did he treat you like that? Sounds like a jerk to me. And you? How pathetic! I have no respect for people who can't move on.

"In short, Ophelia my love, get over him. You've had more time than most to get over this guy. And while you're at it, get over yourself!"

Ophelia raged inside of the body. She had let her power dip too low, the girl was still too powerful. She would leave and find more, then return.

She rose up, then was dragged back down. Sofia had somehow bound her within the body.

"You're not going anywhere," Sofia said. "We're ending this, one way or another, woman to woman. I love Cameron, and he loves me. For real. You know that. I know you know this because I've seen through your eyes. I've been a part of you since the first day, and you've been a part of me." Then her voice softened. "I'm sorry about the way things went with Hamlet. If I'd been around as your friend, you could have cried on my shoulder, and then we would have gone to a club, had a few beers, danced, found a few hot guys and gotten ya laid. Believe me, a much better situation than ending up at the bottom of a swamp."

". . . Laid?" Ophelia asked slowly.

"You know what I'm talking about." Sofia's tone was so sly, Ophelia could almost see the smile, and was instantly embarrassed. "I was with you when you dropped into Shayne."

"Silence!" Ophelia said again, but she spoke as a timid girl, not a raging demon. "Stop it. Leave me alone."

Below them, the woman Claudia had withdrawn the file from Cameron's neck and was meticulously wiping it on his shirt.

"So what'll it be, Ophelia? Are you gonna help me save Cameron, I mean *really* save him? Or are you gonna continue being pouty and selfish." She tried to speak quickly, but calmly. There wasn't much time left. "This isn't a trick. We can't trick each other and we can't abandon each other. Looks like one way or another, we're stuck with each other. And don't worry. I share."

Claudia's hand rose in the air, ready to plunge the file into Cameron's heart.

"Let us restore your love," Ophelia said finally. And their hand shot out, grabbing Claudia by the wrist.

"It lives!" Claudia said, looking up. At first, she was amused. Then she saw the alert look in the black eyes. The mouth working, sputtering out water and mud. Claudia felt fear for the first time.

Words finally became audible.

"Get away from him, you *bitch!*"

Sofia and Ophelia squeezed together with one hand, crushing Claudia's wrist. She screamed in agony and dropped the nail file. With their other hand, they knocked Claudia off of Cameron. She flew headfirst into the balcony doors. They slammed open and she dropped, halfway through across the threshold onto her stomach.

Sofia/Ophelia kneeled beside Cameron. For a brief moment, seeing her face through the blood and pain, he thought she would strangle him again. Then he saw the real Sofia, even through the shark-black eyes, and knew she had returned.

Claudia moaned and started to rise.

Sofia/Ophelia left Cameron and walked toward the older woman. Terrified, Claudia scrambled backward until her back pressed against the stone railing.

"No, get away from me, no!" she cried, bringing her useless hand up to shield her face.

In concert, the two wronged girls guided their hands around the older woman's throat. And began to squeeze, lifting her slowly to a standing position, inexorably pushing her backward so she balanced precariously over the railing.

Just then, Sofia/Ophelia's right hand went completely numb. It fell away from Claudia's throat, limp and lifeless.

"What happened, Ophelia?" Sofia cried.

"I can't—I don't—" Ophelia's voice had suddenly weakened as well, like she was fading, being drawn away.

Rosenberg paused. He had just pinned the body's right arm to the ground. The two sides of the upside-down Y had been stuck in the mud on either side of the girl's wrist. The long part of the branch protruded straight up into the air.

"At least this isn't messy, like crucifixion," he said.

Another shot rang out. This time, a hole appeared in the tarp beside Gyllenhal.

"Let's stake the rest and give ourselves up before they really do kill us."

Rosenberg agreed. Within seconds. Upside-down Ys staked down the remaining limbs.

"Nothing else we can do," Rosenberg said.

"Yes, there is," Gyllenhal said. "A leather strap. Didn't Kay say that was the final piece?"

"Shit, I forgot," Rosenberg said, crestfallen.

"A belt!" Gyllenhal said suddenly. Both lifted their shirts. They were beltless.

"Where'd they go? For crying out loud!" Rosenberg yelled, pacing back and forth in frustration.

"In the hallway, I'd bet." Gyllenhal shrugged.

Rosenberg smiled, "Or under the bed." Gyllenhal smiled back.

"There *that* is then." Gyllenhal slapped his companion on the back. The two turned, hands up, and emerged from the shack slowly.

Claudia saw her chance and clawed at Sofia with her good hand. Moving sluggishly, Sofia only barely avoided losing an eye to the woman's razor sharp nails. Suddenly, Sofia's left hand dropped away, useless. Claudia scrambled to her feet and with one hand, began to haul Sofia over the stone railing of the balcony.

"Ophelia!" Sofia cried.

"Sofia?" Ophelia responded softly, as if from a great distance away. "Let me go, or you'll die."

"I can't—"

Then her legs were gone, paralyzed. She slipped involuntarily down onto the balcony. For a moment, she was free from Claudia's grasp.

"Get up here," Claudia rasped. "I'm not done killing you yet!" She bent to pull Sofia back up again with her good hand.

"Hey, Aunt Claudia!" Cameron blurted out behind her. His voice was thick with blood, but his words were clear.

She turned reflexively, but he had already thrown something. She couldn't dodge it. Whirling like a boomerang, the garden shears flew at her. She put her hands out instinctively to protect herself, but the sharp blades cut through her fingers and embedded themselves in her midsection.

Blood poured out of the irregular stumps as she helplessly tried to grasp the handles.

"Ready to catch the game-winning touchdown pass?" Cameron asked. She looked up. His arm was in motion again. In his hand, Larry's stone.

Cameron threw a bullet, right at the shears. The impact drove the shears even deeper into Claudia. Then she fell backward, flipping over the railing, rock, shears and all. The impact followed barely a second later.

Cameron hobbled over to Sofia, who was lying still on the patio.

"Oh, God, honey. Sofia?"

He cradled her in his lap, but long before that the black tongue protruding from her face, the stillness in her chest, he knew she was gone. Forever.

He rocked her for a few minutes, weeping.

His father was right. He was cursed.

Cameron rested Sofia's head gently against the balcony door and walked back into the room. He opened the chamber door. Harry sat cross-legged in the hallway, facing him. He jumped to his feet immediately.

"Oh, my God, Cam!" he cried at the sight of Cameron's battered face.

Wordlessly, Cameron turned and led Harry back into the room. Harry's hand flew to his mouth when he saw the carnage.

"Aunt Claudia?" Harry asked.

"Mission accomplished," Cameron replied gravely. Then he walked to the balcony, stooped down and kissed Sofia on the lips. Standing, he finally slumped back on the railing, exhausted.

The anniversary clock began to strike twelve.

"You hear that?" he asked Harry. "It's my birthday."

Without a warning, Cameron let himself fall backward and off the balcony.

EPILOGUE

Despite Harry's story of the events in Castle Elsinore, or because of it, the local authorities blamed the large number of bizarre deaths on a group of escaped mental patients. Rosenberg and Gyllenhal had been apprehended by several peat farmers, taken to town, and were quickly released once Harry had told his story. Ophelia's body was reburied, the stakes left as Rosenberg and Gyllenhal had placed them. No one added a leather cord around her neck. The surviving members of Cameron Dean's birthday party returned to the States on the same plane that carried their friends' corpses as cargo.

Eventually, Cameron's inheritance fell under the control of Globe University. They used it to fund new construction and to establish scholarships in the name of Cameron, his parents, and even Claudia Dean.

Castle Elsinore also became a property holding of Globe, often being used for staff retreats or as a hostel for students. Anyone who ever stayed there more than a few nights claimed it was haunted. The most active time was always in mid-November, near Cameron's birthday. At those times, late in the perpetual twilight, voices could be heard, speaking in both English and Danish.

Anyone who had known them recognized that the American voices belonged to Cameron Dean and Sofia Paulsen. The Danish voices were unknown, but always accompanied those of Cameron and Sofia. Only one person ever saw anything, a professor on holiday in Europe who stopped by to admire the castle, and shortly thereafter he quit the university, never to be heard from again.

It is said that he saw the ghosts of Cameron and Sofia walking hand in hand through the castle hallways, happy and laughing. Very much in love. With them was the apparition of a younger girl, flowers in her hair, in medieval garb, also hand in hand with a beau of similar age and dress.

But Cameron and the other boy comprised a single ghost: they shared one pair of legs, joined at the waist like Siamese souls.

Visit the
Simon & Schuster Web site:
www.SimonSays.com

and sign up for our
mystery e-mail updates!

Keep up on the latest
new releases, author appearances,
news, chats, special offers, and more!
We'll deliver the information
right to your inbox — if it's new,
you'll know about it.

POCKET BOOKS   POCKET STAR BOOKS